Crusoe's
Footprint

CARAF Books

•

Caribbean and African Literature
Translated from French

Renée Larrier and Mildred Mortimer, *Editors*

Crusoe's Footprint

PATRICK CHAMOISEAU

TRANSLATED BY JEFFREY LANDON ALLEN AND CHARLY VERSTRAET

Afterword by Valérie Loichot

UNIVERSITY OF VIRGINIA PRESS

CHARLOTTESVILLE AND LONDON

Publication of this translation was assisted by a grant from the
French Ministry of Culture, Centre national du livre.

Originally published in French as *L'empreinte à Crusoé*
© 2012 Éditions Gallimard, Paris

University of Virginia Press
This translation and edition © 2022 by the Rector and Visitors
of the University of Virginia

First published 2022

9 8 7 6 5 4 3 2 1

Library of Congress Cataloging-in-Publication Data

Names: Chamoiseau, Patrick, author. | Allen, Jeffrey Landon, translator. |
    Verstraet, Charly, translator.
Title: Crusoe's footprint / Patrick Chamoiseau ; translated by Jeffrey Landon
    Allen and Charly Verstraet ; afterword by Valérie Loichot.
Other titles: Empreinte à Crusoé. English
Description: Charlottesville : University of Virginia Press, 2022. | Series:
    CARAF books: Caribbean and African literature translated from French |
    Includes bibliographical references.
Identifiers: LCCN 2022026282 (print) | LCCN 2022026283 (ebook) | ISBN
    9780813949055 (hardcover ; acid-free paper) | ISBN 9780813949062
    (paperback ; acid-free paper) | ISBN 9780813949079 (ebook)
Subjects: LCSH: Crusoe, Robinson (Fictitious character)—Fiction. | LCGFT:
    Novels.
Classification: LCC PQ3949.2.C45 E4713 2022 (print) | LCC PQ 949.2.C45
    (ebook) | DDC 843/.914—dc23/eng/20220705
LC record available at https://lccn.loc.gov/2022026282
LC ebook record available at https://lccn.loc.gov/2022026283

The publication of this volume has been supported by *New Literary History.*

Cover art: shutterstock.com/pashabo; shutterstock.com/fran_kie

CONTENTS

Crusoe's
Footprint

*To his Most Serene Highness,
Count Guillaume Pigeard de Gurbert,
Just like that, ever as close,*
But without philosophy.*

---

* "Ever as close," *tout contre*, is probably a reference to Pigeard's work *Contre la philosophie*.

I believe it is impossible to express, to the life, what the ecstasies and transports of the soul are, when it is so saved, as I may say, out of the very grave.

—DANIEL DEFOE, *Robinson Crusoe*

And my solitude not only threatens the foundation of all things, it undermines the very foundation of their existence.

—MICHEL TOURNIER, *Vendredi ou Les limbes du Pacifique*

Thus is genesis extinguished and destruction unheard of.

—PARMENIDES, *The Poem*

Let us start by acknowledging impenetrability.

—VICTOR SEGALEN

There is no hinterland. You cannot hide behind your face.

—ÉDOUARD GLISSANT

How colossal a task is the inventory of reality.

—FRANTZ FANON

Captain's Log

July 22—In the year of our Lord 1659—These journeys to the New World never cease to surprise me, and God knows how many I have led over these last twenty years. At the first streak of dawn, we reached a sea of sparkling blue algae that shimmered pink onto the sky and the low-hanging clouds. After the storm we had just weathered, it was as if we were entering a world, alight with wonder, where reality began to softly quiver . . .

A soft wind blew, yet I eased the sails so that the crew could experience this moment so unusual. Everyone leaned over the rail, some climbed the ropes or clumped together on the observation post, and in a stunned, quasi-sacred silence, we contemplated this wonder that our ship was ever so slowly dividing . . .

We shall soon reach Saint-Domingue and then Brazil, the ship's hold is silent, there was no screaming, just the dreadful smell that I tried to fight once again with warm vinegar and richly aromatic herbs . . .

1

THE IDIOT

my lord, I was born once again into the year I knew nothing of, in this time of equinox on my forgotten island, probably at the same moment when I felt as though I was slipping between two bodies of light; one from the glistening of the ocean, and the other formed by the unrelenting phosphorescence of the beach; between the two was not only my body, my parasol, my animal pelt rags, my clicking musket, or even the saber that was hitting my leg from the bottom of the shoulder harness; no; it was also the conceit of body and mind that summed up those twenty years of solitude during which I had successfully subdued the misfortune despite everything;

I had moved toward this side of the island after feeling safe from harm for some time; I believed I had reached the final stage of law and order from which nothing could have brought me back; I had appeased the demons of the blood, the flesh, and the mind, tamed fears, and defeated these regressions that many a time had me sprawled like a pitiful toad in backwater; moreover; I had retained the gift of speech; and even the ability to write; and despite never clearly understanding this strange little book that survived the wreck of the old frigate, I opened it day after day, longed to flip through it, made a habit of reading it, and practiced this liturgy in order to often rewrite its enigmatic sentences at random;

It had been a long time since I had come back to the place where I had first set foot on the autumnal equinox, inaugurating, unknowingly at the time, the eternity of a tragedy that had been deprived of witnesses; forgetting this beach had been my way of casting off the hope of departing from this place, the pain and sorrow of possibly returning; thus I had expressed my formal desire to deal with the island, my solitude, my despair, my memory lapses, and tears, and to forge a destiny out of it by way of hard work, order, and reason; as soon as I could, I had therefore turned my back on these fretful years spent looking out for a sail in these salty waters that gave the sky its leaden appearance; my first years were filled battling the hope of being visited, as well as dreading it for fear of native cannibals in the area; one day without a second thought, I up and deserted that shore, first to distance myself from that beach and its vain hopes, and then to explore the heart of the island and finally grab it by the horns; careful not to fear like before, I had stopped considering this place for plotting or grazing, and removed it from my grand endeavors of civilization; I never used to come here; I hardly touched this place, thus condemning it to indigent wilderness; and this pride anew, this appeasement that finally allowed me to devise some happiness, enabled me to come back with the fervor of a great lord, with no trouble or fear, just the satisfaction of apprehending, in one panoramic view, the dramatic point of departure and the splendor of what I had managed to become;

after all these years, I can say that I was happy then, without any vain hopefoolness, without the scab of a single regret, simply impeccable within my sovereign order over this scrap of land; I serenely contemplated my future; the thought of dying here no longer frightened me; I remembered that this outlook was a recurring concern; passing away on this island meant surrendering my body to the red ants and hairy crabs that disgusted me so; the image of my body decaying this way overwhelmed me with a sense of a perfect damnation; I had therefore created, among my numerous great foundations, a cemetery—emphatically baptized: "*Memorial to the Human*"; I had placed it on a rocky hill, and on windy, arid, sunburned despair where even a worm would not survive, and was therefore naturally inaccessible to those bubbles of pus that develop on carcasses; and it is there that I dug myself a hole, lined with translucent cotton, and beside it, I wove some wood to form a railing to prevent the rocks from cascading; after lying at the bottom of the vault, I would be free to carry out my entombment with a vine that triggered a small mechanism; the rocks would then cover me for all eternity while a mast, hoisted by a loose strap, would have waved in all directions to announce the place of my sepulcher; an epitaph would be hidden at the foot of my cross, displaying my existence and my own misfortune; from then on, I had watched out for the smallest drop in my vital signs just under the onset of fever, the insidious softening of my body or mind; were I to have the slightest hint, I stayed close to my tomb long enough to heal, ready to lie down in case the icy edge of the great Scythe were to harvest my soul; I had known many a moment of despair when I welcomed thoughts of ending it all, but the simple idea of giving up my soul to such solitude, so far from every possibility, infused me with the courage to carry on; today, I had forgotten where my tomb was; dying here no longer scared me; a considerable part of the island had become my work, a beautiful piece of art, in which my death could be inscribed with dignity in the face of scavengers; life has meaning only when lived to the fullest; being neither animal, nor one of these savages that infested the world; that, I had achieved; I had become a founder of civilization; and on this beach of beginning, I wanted to proclaim it in the face of all these dragons of light and to this monster of green power that was the island;

*

back at the starting point, the question of my origin occurred to me; I still did not know how, when, or why I had landed here; I had imagined being a survivor of the shipwreck I had discovered in the jaws of the cays, a few hundred yards away from the place where I had awakened; a frigate I had explored and plundered like an Oriental cave, like a chronicle of the Western world, a relic of all humanity, that had given me the means to start, or start over; but no matter how much I searched the remnants of the memorial—books, parchment papers, or ledgers that had turned to dust over the years—I had never found anything that could explain what I was doing here, or why I was here, where I came from and most importantly who I was;

there had been an intense period during which I had begun to search the frigate; the shipwreck turned out to have so many tools, weapons, images, and various utensils that it quickly became the tabernacle of a highly desired world, filling my imagination; water had flooded three-fourths of the wreckage; sand had filled the bottom parts; the hold remained inaccessible, but where I was able to rummage at my leisure—before a sudden storm could return it to oblivion—I had found things to . . . rebuild civilization . . . truly, a whole set of behaviors, values, and attitudes that emerged from these thousands of objects; at first, in order to define from whence I had come, I had conducted a veritable examination of these things, looking for clues on each one, names, places, lines of descent; nothing that I had discovered could unequivocally trace back to me; I then hopelessly stumbled upon a small coffer of necromancies and divinations; it was full of little crystal balls, and strips of fabric with spells used for incantations all over them, cards, dice, cowrie shells, magic wands, potions, powders, flasks, and loads of abracadabra that I could not figure out how to use; abiding by the instructions of a water-damaged textbook, I had put on some clothes that happened to be on board and that in this case could only belong to those passed-on souls; I had added a large white cloth that I collected in the front forecastle, the sort of shroud used during funerals for throwing bodies overboard on the high seas; I had eaten black, unleavened bread for ten days, a bit doughy and full of salt; I had slept on a carpet of dead crabs; I had swallowed small scavengers replete with the flesh of the cadavers; I had burned incense and placed very complex arrangements made of bird bones around me; then I had called out to the dead, the spirits, and the specters that must have been roaming about the sinister frigate; after I had asked them multiple questions entangled with appropriate spells, I had begun listening to their signs and advice; I was met only with bleak silence, at times with an abysmal mustiness, suggesting that I was now well beyond all reality, in a place where the power of the dead itself left no possible access to chance whatsoever;

*

the only possibility that I could make out (like a crack in an invisible wall) came from the shoulder harness that I had found tangled in my legs upon awakening; it had wrapped around a piece of the boat's stem, mooring me, consequently turning it into an improvised life preserver; this coincidence had no doubt kept me safe from being crushed by the cays and from various debris whirling around until I was propelled, with no soul or memory, into the sea foam on the beach; before the silence of the dead, I was forced to hold and cling on to this lone harness;

the harness bore an inscription on one of the embroidered straps; a seal of ownership, in red ochre calligraphy; a name, a man's name; since I had not found a single bloody crew member in the gangways or the cabins, or between the planks of the deck; in the days following, all that was left were half-eaten, half-decomposed corpses thrown onto the beach by the storms; nothing about them was recognizable, be it identity or humanity; I was decidedly the only surviving thing capable of carrying on the human name; suffering from the distressed gulf of my memory, I would eventually take on a name; but from where? ... naturally, from the inscription with no origin or designation: Robinson Crusoe;

for twenty years, this inscription became a book whose pages I had to fill; not so much a declaration of my own identity, but rather a commitment to existence, like a path to follow on the frightening topography of the island; I took delight in it many times over, crying, yelling, vomiting, smiling, sometimes dozing, in surges of madness or sweet melancholy; and it was this name that I repeated to myself once again that morning, but in a peaceful and natural serenity that was in tune with my state of mind; *my name is Robinson Crusoe, and I am lord of this place;*

the mystery of my origin had tortured me for quite some time, but the torment of my survival quickly took the upper hand; I was even a bit surprised to see this questioning arise while on a simple pilgrimage to the initial landing; in this gap that served as my memory, something was still troubling me, as it had always done in each of my introspections; it was not the details surrounding my origin, nor its very truth; I felt that it was linked to something unbearable, *an immense pain,* and that constituted (more so than the desire for any direct line of descent) the place of impact of a past within me, indecipherably inscribed; I bore the suffering without knowing what it could be, especially since I kept trying to convince myself that the origin didn't matter—what mattered was being Robinson Crusoe, only master after God, and lord of this island;

*

my newfound nobility layered with twenty years of survival was thus incorporated into this embroidery; two words, one name, nothing more than a trace without heraldry; I told myself that it was nice to have no origin; I had assumed the identity of this majesty without spectator, and it suited me well; because of the absence of origin, what I had become rose up within me, flowing from no lineage, no bloodline, and the first stage of being born again was fulfilled at the exact moment when I awakened as a castaway on that cursed beach;

*

waking up . . . in pain . . . my lacerated consciousness now suddenly a blazing torch; I had looked around me not understanding where I was, then the terrible reality of this island had splashed upon every one of my flattened perceptions; it is then that those long years began to terrorize me, at times more vividly than others . . . but let's return, my lord, to the moment of impact . . .

I had come to, dizzy and distraught, woeful and feverish, incapable of understanding where I was; the sun was setting someplace, in the luminescence that, due to my distress, was transformed into visions of fire in a forge on this plant-covered monster that was this island; seized by terror was I at the idea of winding up in a place that the oldest of sailors dread, a place where thousands of ships and crew are never to be seen again; no matter how wide I opened my eyes, I had no point of reference, everything was strange, as foreign as death is to life; I would need to strain both my eyes and my mind to even begin to understand what I was perceiving; terror multiplied to the point of horror, be it the tiniest rustling of leaves, the tiniest movement of crustaceans, or the mixture of chirps of invisible insects and peculiar birds; my stunned eyes distorted the smallest shape into grimacing vampires, every pointed tip becoming a fang; every curve turned into claws; shapeless forms became a demonic fermentation or a swarm of devouring slime; the sea standing before me, licking me with its acid foam, was reduced to a gurgling tasked with absorbing living things from recent storms; and the air was laden with the odor of dead algae that haloed hurricanes and remains long after, a fitting smell for total despair;

after taking refuge in a tree, I had wrapped myself around the thinnest branch, as close to the tip as my weight would allow; I had turned my back to the sky and directed my awareness to the threat that is the ground, scrutinizing the foliage, every detail noted through one dilated pupil as the darkening night commanded; I had spent that whole entire night on the lookout quailing and vomiting, feeling dragons brush up against me, as well as ghouls or lwas seemingly crawling over me; at sunrise, I found myself distraught with fatigue and fear, hanging lopsided on the brittle branch, and I had almost tumbled thirty feet down, so frightened at nearly being sent straight to the devil;

*

my first morning consisted of walking the beach, with worried steps, with careful steps, and with hopeless steps; as I was feeling feverish, I made a concoction of rum and tobacco, sipping on it for several minutes while also rubbing it all over my body before hiding away someplace for the night; turning my back to an island that I cared nothing for, this place seemed both deceased and threatening, deserted yet teeming; I tried to forget about it and focus only on the spectacle of the sea, hoping for that mysterious ship that had brought me here; so the days passed; I don't know how many identical days, how many weeks I would attempt the colossal task of pacing the beach with deep longing, shaking from hunger, blistering from thirst; at my weakest, I forced down shellfish or soft algae, my devout tongue disinfecting it just before swallowing; for fear of not being in the right place, I allowed myself thirty cubits to leave and come back to the exact spot where I had awoken; this obsessive wandering eventually furrowed several inches into the sand; it established a barrier between the sea foam and the island, radiating so much anguish that even the crabs stayed away from it; gigantic turtles coming to nest turned around abruptly when they reached the line; yet this desperate circuit would eventually extend to carry me as far as the tip of the headland and this is how, out of nowhere, I spotted the frigate: it lay like a city, clearly old and bygone, among the sharp cays, and emitted these waves of sadness that even the oldest of sailors would say predicted the appearance of real ghost ships; short-lived then was my relief; this ship was the only thing that could have transported me to this wretched place; yet, the wreck seemed a thousand years old: the sails tattered, the depressing cordage now all but spiderwebs frayed by ancestral winds; I had fallen to my knees in the sand, not only in total despair, but also thrust into a spiral of im-possible, when my mind lost all sense of balance;

*

this serious failure to understand came in two blows: on the one hand, there was the enigma of being beached in such a place; on the other hand, there was the feeling of having been there since the dawn of time like the sand or the crabs; the turmoil of being or not being from here, threatened from the outside and seized from within, this feeling will ever remain part of the foundation of my tragic existence on this hopeless island; there wasn't a single bird, creature, leaf, or fruit, literally nothing familiar to me; each detail was a cry of funereal hostility; the sky acted as a lid and the sea a wall, their boundaries eventually becoming indistinguishable to the point of forming a prison with invisible bars that had bound to each fiber of my being;

*

very quickly, I had shielded myself against this hostile power; I had set about making a provisional cave dwelling for myself by rearranging a landslide of large volcanic rocks, between which the roots of three cursed fig trees had taken hold; I then spent weeks amassing what I could bring back from the frigate before it abruptly vanished; around this makeshift shelter I had erected fences of bamboo, reinforced with thorns so as to ward off the wild, bloodthirsty beasts that were presumably roaming around; day by day, I had continued to be on safeguard, never straying far from the beach, nor from these piles of dry wood, destined to go up in smoke the second a sail materialized on the horizon; in order to do this, I had laid out amadou as tinder, some black powder, and a flint around each pile; I made my way to the frigate on a raft of sappy wood secured with vines much like hemp when dry; I loaded the raft as much as I could, then paddled intensely back to shore so as to quickly escape being sucked back into the cays; I stopped at nightfall only to begin again at daybreak; at times, I found myself stuck on the frigate: shark fins crisscrossing the path; other times, the large rays with their dark wings shaped like devils would loiter about the wreckage; I awaited the departure of these evils before returning with my loot which made landfall in complete shambles along the beach; *cordage, bits of sail, twibills, hammers, nails, rabbet planes, caps, chain pieces, sabers, harpoons, powder kegs, mallets, muskets, pistols, an oil dispenser, hammocks, large canvas tents, string, needles, barrels of dry biscuits, chisels, casks of rum, scalpels, flasks of various grains, salt shakers, forks, clogs, breeches, trunks, padlocked chests and safes* . . . such an accumulation of objects made me feel infinitely better, as if between this island and me stood a comforting rampart; I continued this frenzy for objects, some collected by greed, before contemplating how outlandishly they sprawled over dozens of yards, tallying them one by one in my head . . . *awls, teapots, sugar bowls, sponges, sets of keys, drafting triangles, spyglass, a soup tureen, jewelry boxes, hardware and scrap metal, brushes, small cannonballs, shears, flat files, arquebuses, chassepots, small cases, round files, cartridge boxes, plates and mess kits, crucifix . . .* ;

but on top of this incessant transit and initial fortification, I all the while began to forge a piece of armor as internal and humane as possible; my eyes gazed along the horizon in hopes of spotting a sail, imagining a father, a mother, brothers and sisters, a village someplace in the world; I was inventing a group of ancestors that would have bequeathed these shambles to me; I was populating the outskirts of the beach with a crowd of customary demons and a lineage of gods to watch over my cradle . . . ; on this foundation, I started to inhabit my name, *Robinson Crusoe,* to dig a place for myself; the objects brought back from the frigate nourished my imagination with a Western perspective: I was a prince, Castilian, knight, dignitary of great table, officer of legions; I roamed from castle to castle, manor gardens, walking through large rooms that were draped in velvet; wandered across filthy cobblestones, in streets turned yellow from the oil lanterns; walking along fields of wheat that undulated endlessly at the foot of high ramparts . . . ; but strange images suddenly emerged from memory lapses: a disarray of dark forests dripping with moss, cities made of soil haloed by ashes and jasmine, sand dunes as far as the eye could see, cliffs covered in black birds flapping their ashen wings; or rather the cry of women mixed with both the pain of death and songs of joy . . . ; many a strange thing seemingly from my inner self added to this—*. . . a jackal's arrival that troubles the gods . . . black and white lizards that weave cloths . . . twins in a millet calabash . . . bracelets of priests clinking against the sides of a horned mask . . .*—but they were so incompatible with the rest of my evocations that I attributed them to residual memories belonging to some boastful sailor I had allegedly met; in fact, reconstructing my imagination from these objects bound to my obscure memory led only to chaos: any possibility of demystifying my origins would then disappear;

*

be that as it may, these illusions must not have been convincing; confronted with this hostile power that constituted this island and its surroundings, low morale was not uncommon considering my lack of origins; leaving all consistency aside, I fancied myself a crab, an octopus in an octopus hole, the young of octopuses in a consortium of octopuses; I found myself playing toadpole in the bubbles of the sludge; but the worst part arose when I reached the immutable point of being absent from myself; my gaze would then settle upon nothing, it captured solely the luminous halo of the things around me; I began to sniff, to grunt, and to lend my ear toward my surroundings; in those moments, I stumbled along, drooling from my open mouth, and I felt better when my hands mirrored the long strides of my feet; then I came to (God knows how!) and, to safeguard a remnant of humanity, I returned to these narrative fevers that possessed my mind for many long years; I found nothing better to do than to invent my own story, weaving it into a legend; I wrote it on the faded pages of a few thick ledgers salvaged from the frigate, longing to secure this legend within me, within a desire's reach; it must certainly have sprung from one or two great books still buried in my mind; books already written by others yet I had only to rewrite, to unwrite, having only to increase the space between lines, between words and realities, to fill them with what I was unwittingly becoming, and what I aspired to become even though I was incapable of articulating it;

over the early years of my rebirth, I had thereby always revealed the civilized individual I imagined being, and the human sanctified in spoken or written word that I strived to be; on all corners of the island, out of this little book came words, sentences, verses that would signal, indicate, designate, remind, exorcise, label, repeat, invoke . . . : *Pleasure Grounds . . . Companions of Immortal Coachmen . . . Path of Yearning Dignity . . . This is a fact: to be is . . . Place of Memories . . . Courage . . . Chapel of Peace . . . The Way of the Word, which leaves only: there is . . . Harmony and Courage . . . Basilica of Return . . . that he be absolutely, or not at all . . . Prayers . . . Arch of Providence . . . ;*

I assigned them all to my will to live, not only to retain a language in this sordid solitude that only came out as a growl, but especially in my desire to preserve writing at all costs that—more than the Word—was perfectly useless here;

but quickly did I become aware that this solitude affected my speech after all, distorted my internal language, obscuring my writing that would never be read; let us say then that between this prison-like island and myself I was reduced to raising an extraordinary amount of signs and symbols behind which I moved as I pleased, and which I interpreted with equally as much liberty; crosses and triangles, circumpuncts, letters, and numbers that flowed from my hand to dress my dwellings or to adorn my habitual paths; I used all that to support my mental health and to simultaneously compose an intelligible landscape for myself; this obstinacy to preserve a form of "expression" represented for me the essence of the true-human; without a second thought I repeated these actions, but this intuition grew valuable: I now knew that one is shaped also by his "expression," with which one stands; I was delighted with that;

at the beginning of all origins is the word; over the course of these twenty years, I had slowly rediscovered it; very quickly, I had the very naive awareness to develop my creative word, with total freedom, and in all likelihood at the cost of a slow stupefaction of what I could or would express; but "expression" is not meant to be understood (just like all literature I suppose)—its initial use is to construct the authority of the one who activates it; this is why, over these twenty years, I had wielded air and substance (in order to write), I had marked the ground with it, I had made pollen in the wind from it, tattooed the skin of the rains, the bark of cinnamon trees and the light of full moons, populated my nightmares and my sleepless fevers; at my most stable, I was satisfied with transcribing my "expression" on my faded books, in the contractions of meanings that sometimes became signs and then constituted the only beacons in my mind to retain a foundation;

this burning "expression" was inscribed in a wider practice which was that of rituals; there is no humanity without rituals, and even if many animals also perform numerous rites, no human mind goes about its misery without the crutch of a ritual; but the ones I implemented were in no way part of the same tribe as those obscure ceremonies that savages perform; thus each dawn of these past two decades triggered a luminous mechanism for me; first, upon waking, I greeted the beginning of the day with open arms by reciting one of these enigmatic sentences from my dear little book:

> *... when the daughters of the Sun,*
> *who had abandoned the palaces of the Night,*
> *ran toward the light while in my procession,*
> *their hands moving aside the veils that concealed their heads ...*

then I rang the bell which awakened my goats, my guinea rats, roused my parrots, and the rest of my domesticated fauna; and then, all the while master and servant, with gestures worthy of wigs and gloves, I prepared my hors d'œuvres, cheese, soursop, buckwheat crepes and goat milk, and cassava bread; and I settled under my large kapok tree, on these bound planks that serve as a main table; it was always a delight for me to take out embroidered tablecloths, Asian porcelain, hallmarked silverware, carafes from Aubagne that held rainwater, and a whole protocol of utensils made of silver whose only utility lay in the pleasure of imagining the hands of the women who had touched them; after this light meal, I proceeded to hoist my little flag, it too covered in sentences whose meanings I could not decide upon; then came the reading of the Constitution that I had written very long ago—a text that solemnized so many fundamental rules that pronouncing them daily established a rampart between me and this island; right after the Constitution came the utterance of a series of guidelines—such as *"Always keep the chin higher than the clavicle," "Do not hold your mouth open," "Eating is done while seated at a table and on a chair," "The back is stretched and is extended in vertical alignment with the*

sun," "One shall not break wind as it is only fitting for animals,"
"Continually observe and speak to yourself so as to maintain
posture . . ."; as well as: *"God exists," "The devil can be charm-*
ing," "Joy is here!," "Meditate on one's honor each time upon
seeing a red fruit," "Meditate on one's dignity each time upon
seeing a yellow fruit," "The earth is round and every island drift-
ing from its crust lands somewhere . . ."; I also recited a few ar-
ticles from my Penal Code, three from my Civil Code, six from
my Trade Legislation; I outlined a few graphs from my cadastral
plan, and I recalled aloud the principles of this civic service to
which I must adhere for every new moon . . . ; it is impossible to
enunciate it all to you; their infinite profusion was constituent
of their very purpose; their number had more value than what
they efficiently ordered; added to this was a bunch of procedures about animals, pastures, fields, restoration tasks, periods
of writing and reading in the little book . . . ; a framework of
unchanging acts which had illuminated my sad existence as a
human-island on this prison of an island; my rituals had multiplied day by day, until my mental space, but also the entire
island, disappearing under their authority, was revealed to my
awareness in a hardly domesticated form . . . ;

*

upon reflection, I told myself occasionally that over the millennia
the scepter of civilization was transmitted from chosen people
to chosen people, thus reinforcing itself, now it had fallen upon
me—upon me, all by myself!—without really knowing from
which end to grasp it; I had taken it out from the frigate, and
brandishing it as I could, feeling as though this time it would
concern only myself; but, as years passed, I came to understand
that this scepter had probably known individual periods, and
that, even in the most miserable of its adventures, the issue of
humanity would ever be the one hurled into the contingency of
this vast game; this burden had often made me stand tall; and
terrified me just as much; I was somehow chosen;

*

the days and years had engulfed each other this way, one after the other, and the nights amounted to nothing more than
a steady stream of nightmares; when I could no longer lie in
my bed of dry leaves, captured by the almighty island forebod-
ingly staring down upon me, I sat upright on a table made of
wood from a gum tree; at night I wrote there, illuminated by
small candles made from vampire grease that I collected from
the bark of a moaning tree; as light, the candles released a reddish soot that bestowed upon my writing—my remnants of
humanity—a constant quavering—concerning and therefore
precious fragility . . . ;

*

there had been a time when I had stopped wallowing in self-
pity; I had been devoted, in body and soul, to these rituals that
day by day called for more and more of them; I had proclaimed
new measures and had carried them out pronto; my profound
joy was to see them abundant around me, standing up to this
malevolent island; no more need to know who or what I was,
there was only the island, its hostile mass and its dangers; above
it, the metallic mass of the sky seemed so unbearable that I had
spent many seasons projecting divinities of the sun or wind at it,
divining sirens in the clouds to lure boats; storms had only been
rumbling damnations from some kind of monster, and the most
peaceful moon had never been anything else than the lifeless
eye of a jailer; sometimes, I had given up on this magical spirit
for a bit of reason, thus striving to use scientific observations
in order to predict violent rains or devastating cyclones; in this
same way, I had sanctioned many studies fueled by the desire of
determining the exact point when rainy season turned to dry;
but this line navigated with such variance, causing me to always
return to the feeling that some indecisive goddess was behind all
of this; in my struggle with the sky, I had however learned how
to contemplate it in its cold hostility, having nothing come of
it, and having no reason to expect anything from it; and I had
ensured that the absence of any benevolence did not affect my
mood whatsoever;

I had proceeded similarly with the sea—or rather with this wall of phosphorescence and hysterical moods—that I had begged so many times and filled with so many imaginary boats coming to my rescue; I had wanted to make it an ally by hollowing out the trunk of a gum tree to make a broad pirogue, whose sides I had widened with broad flames so as to hold them up with bolsters; I had stabilized it as best as possible with a few bamboo poles per a technique learned from savages I must have met in my forgotten past; I had also sculpted ironwood paddles, and had prepared long rods to guide me through the cays; I had even spent time sewing sections of the sails and planned to attach them to a makeshift mast with a very ingenious cordage system; all of this had maintained an insane hope within me for the better part of a year, and it seemed as though the ocean kindly gave me hope; the problem had been that the felled gum tree was located seven leagues from the beach; even if I were able to stubbornly slide it over more than two leagues in less than a season, I had come across an immense volcanic bomb overlooking a gully; an obstacle like this required such an effort of circumvention that it was relegated to the category of painful tasks, the ones that, even with considerable progress, would remain forever unfinished, alas; yet, I only really surrendered this project upon discovering that the sunlight was causing my pirogue to sprout voracious plants, and I also realized how rooted the flank was from resting on the ground; thus, the ocean abandoned all sympathy;

so, over the years and through my resignation, the sea also devolved into a venomous abyss with no kindness—per my maritime laws, a jungle to rule over sharks, jellyfish, and stinging seaweed; each new moon, I stood tall on one of those headlands, the ocean crashing below as if it wanted to swallow the island, and I kept it at bay by way of a great deal of proclamations, decrees, letters patent, and advanced police measures, all accompanied by uncompromising edicts; for example, article 7 of my Maritime Code forbade all waves to display as black or dark, only light indigo or jade green were tolerated; I put storms in order, forcing them to be declared in advance, and

I set a strict distance on how far they could advance inland; I dealt with boxfish catching, barring entry to venomous fish, crab distribution, turtle invasions, shipwreck possession, or treasures that the waves were authorized to deposit without taxation . . . ; I established very strict measures on debarkation matters of anything at all, forcing all immigrant groups to comply with entry regulations and a mandatory quarantine of at least thirty days . . . ; after establishing my expectations of the sea, I must admit that I had subjected it to the severity of a fierce dictatorship, as well as irrevocably confining it to the limits and toxin of its great hatred toward me . . . ; alas, when I was able to accept the hostility of the sky, to contemplate the sea without petition, no longer expecting a sail to appear, while having hoped to see nothing other than that some type of sail would appear; well, at that very moment, without realizing it, the idea of humanity and its existence had sunk, leaving no trace within me;

here's how I went on to discover it . . .

*

I thus made my way down that cursed beach, ruminating on my glory, when suddenly something unusual caught my attention; the beach was teeming—not to say alive for I still hesitated to confer any tolerable life to this island—, with each step, one encountered crumbs of shipwrecks, residue of drowned cities, stone and pieces of grit from churches or tiny pearls in the gills of dead fish; in the first moments of my rigid reclusion, millennial cadavers kept suddenly appearing at the frigate's flanks; even after all these years, I still expected to stumble over one of them, still unidentifiable, that is to say a mass of bones in disarray within an immortal gelatin that the sun forced to crackle into thousands of bubbles; these discoveries had greatly affected me at the beginning, and later less and less; I also remember that in the beginning I took care to dig these corpses a grave in the sand, until discovering that the sea always scoured them and departed with its grim loot; I also discovered that countless vulturous beings delighted in these fermentations and transformed the improvised tombs into indecent concentrations of voracities; in the end, I circumvented the remains that the sea continually returned, abandoning them to the mercy of the sand; they disappeared very quickly, dried from exposure to the sun, carted around by the nomadic crabsortium, dissolved like cuttlefish, leaving only the haze of souls that I caught sight of gallivanting above the octopuses among the almond trees . . . ;

despite the assault from these old memories, my gaze remained vigilant, scrutinizing each detail of this hostile beach; as I approached, things escaped from the phosphorescent blur, flickering and catching my eye, and then were suddenly revealed to my serene gaze; and this is how I saw it;

a shape, unusual, part of the sand but solidified as if someone had wanted to preserve it; before I even understood what it was, my heart sank in the bustle of a disaster; my legs vanished; I fell to my knees; I nearly had to crawl in order to make my way toward this unsettling shape; I began to observe it as one would look at a world in its entirety; it was neither turtle tracks, nor the impression from a small manatee's nap; I wanted to convince myself that a large bird had touched down there and had slipped because of a certain something, and it had created this singular shape; I also thought about the legend of the she-devils that tricked people by altering their hooves' impact so that it remained indecipherable; in a few half-seconds, I considered millions of possibilities; they scrolled through my mind with the slimy force of a jellyfish tide; then, while my poor heart skipped a beat, that icy sweat plowed my skin, I eventually saw . . . a heel . . . the curve of the arch of a foot . . . the distribution typical of a set of toes . . . and each toe rushing through my mind setting off alarms and threats, anger and hatred, threats; all of it though mixed with the inexplicable breath of a terrifying enthusiasm: it was a human footprint;

*

my first impulse was to take refuge in the closest tree; but, while grabbing hold of the trunk, I remembered that first night, and I did not want to relive the same torments; I rushed into the thick woods where I began to run as if I were possessed, without really knowing if it was toward the south, the north, or the east; I had lost my hat, my parasol, my pistols, and my musket; as for the large saber that tapped against my thigh, it had become so entangled in my shins that I cast it aside to the devil without breaking my stride; I squeezed into a shady gully named *Thermal Baths of Eternal Youth;* there was a spring that I had skillfully converted, with a fence, a swing made of green vines, slabs of pink rock, and bamboo canals; like a crab dug deep into its hole, I remained motionless, panting like a bear as quickly as the cool water gurgled; once my mind calmed, I reflected once more upon what I had seen; the footprint was going inward from the beach; someone must have landed during the night, and had rushed inland; maybe a squad; how many footprints? . . . I had only seen one; the sea must have washed the rest of them away; the pirogue that had brought them here must have been hidden under the cover of the almond trees; I was kicking myself, had I paid closer attention, I could have located it right away; I could have had a better idea of what I was dealing with; how many were there?—ten? a hundred? a thousand? a horde?—I could not stop ruminating over it; my body trembled as if I had tertian fever, and my eyelids blinked uncontrollably; my arms were crossed across my chest, and my hands convulsing safely inside my armpits . . . ;

*

it is impossible to tell how many hours I spent this way; I believe the night came and went, the day finding me in the same position and in the same state; proceeding with extreme caution, it took me quite some time to emerge from the gully; motionless in a tuft of gigantic mushrooms, I devoted nearly an hour to examining the surroundings in case of an ambush; like a scalded rat, I dashed back to the cave that served as a dwelling, at the foot of the giant kapok tree, at the back of my tent and huts; once sheltered behind the fence, I brought my six ladders back, I blocked the small drawbridge with provisional stones, the three posterns, and the two nail-studded portcullises; I closed the arrow slits concealed in the thorny hedge that I had densely planted directly against the fence; and once again, unable to even think, I hid away deep within my cave, in a seeping cavity that served no purpose until now; this is where I felt safe, in the fetal position, incapable of repressing the shivers of terror that had transformed me into a whiny brat;

it was as if these twenty years of pretentious falsehoods were suddenly torn away and had brought me back to my weak hopes, to my initial fears, and to my former anguish—*someone other than me was now on the island! . . .*—it could not be civilized people; it was not the print of a boot or clog; moreover, no ship was to be found on the horizon; back on the beach, I walked down the shore where no rowboat or skiff was to be seen; the one or ones who had landed here could only be native cannibals from the region; I was incapable of situating this island, but in the back of my mind, I knew that places as desperate as these could only be infested with ogres, ghouls, demons, and a large pack of cannibals; no matter how I tried to repress the images in my mind, I could already see them subjecting my body to the worst rituals; I could practically see them unrolling my bowels and mixing them with spices; slices of my thigh combined with fermented bark; sensual dances wherein one of these beasts tried to swallow my eyeballs . . . ; I seemingly heard drums beating, identical to those I had perceived the nights I had first come ashore; naturally, the days broke with such burden that I could not remain devoted to my rituals whatsoever; days came and went such that I could not keep track; I was neither hungry nor thirsty, no desire for anything; transfixed, petrified, or agitated like an old poisoned cat; other times, I would lose myself, but it was even worse: I made cannibals out to be far more revolting without my consciousness to temper it somewhat;

*

I suffered a moment of great weakness, during which I could not remain seated, or even folded in the fetal position; I was simply thrown on the ground, limp, listless, my bones throbbing in my temples; in this turmoil, I heard the din from my baby goats, pigs, billy goats, moorhen, guinea fowls, and parrots, who were hungry, thirsty, and who over this endless time period had not been looked after; their distress helped me find a reason to stand up; moreover, an alarm in my mind signaled to me that this hullabaloo would undoubtedly attract savages; they would barge into my sanctuary and would have no problem eating me alive; I dragged myself to a barrel of dry biscuits that I had made from my own wheat; I carefully nibbled on them; I waited to recover a semblance of energy, and with incalculable caution, I crawled through the darkness of the cave toward the halo of the opening; then I slipped into the glare of light that overwhelmed the entrance; once outside, the inner space around the kapok tree seeming peaceful, I rushed into one of the gatehouses of the fence to look around; all looked normal; I returned to the depths of the cave to make myself some new guns, knives, and a saber; I added a nasty blunderbuss that I hung across my back; I filled a calabash with small lead rounds and another with black powder; then, through a series of quick strides interspersed with moments of attention, I went to meet my domesticated animals in all the pens, enclosures, gardens, and pastures; I gave them water and bundles of fresh herbs; I handed them fruits, soft peels, and all sorts of grains; I dispersed rats that were feasting in the fields of barley, wheat, rice, and potatoes . . . ; furtive and uneasy, I carried out what I had practiced imperially each day of these last twenty eternities; calm returned very quickly to most of my estates; a silence of order and discipline was reinstituted; I somehow felt soothed;

*

fortified by this restoration of order, I began inspecting my estates for seven leagues around; caution advised me to avoid my usual routes; forgetting marks and paths, I sneaked along the gullies that rain hollows out at the bottom of those gigantic trees; I climbed knotted roots, similar to witches' castles, and I walked along clumping bamboo whose creaks made me think of children sighing; I crawled under curtains of fern to go around the exposed fields, and, always under cover, always crouched in a fitting shadow, I examined the surroundings, watching for any indication of movement, or any sign of tracks; from afar I inspected the state of the edges that protected my vegetable garden and my medicinal plants; I looked over my plots of aloe, melons, coffee, wild sugarcane; I checked those trays where I dried seagrapes, wicker for basketry, tobacco leaves, and thin fish . . . ; I monitored my bamboo pipes, my small wind turbines that kept me abreast of matters of the wind, my lime kiln where I fired seashells to reinforce my fence, and my coal stoves, and my lumberjacking areas where felled trees awaited ripening in order to become planks; I lingered over blooming orchids that I gathered beneath shade houses for aesthetic pleasure . . . ; I searched my official huts one after the other, *Police Station, Customs, Department of Weights and Measures, Office of Land Registry, Office of Coastlines and Borders, Heritage Museum, Department of Defense, Institute of Natural Sciences, School of Cartography* . . . they were more often empty than not, with a stool, a writing desk, a candle, a duck quill, a calabash bowl filled with fish ink, a relic of registry, and a few shelves awaiting the deeds and official statements; normally, I sat in each office, taking turns, according to a seasonal procedure largely unchanged, and I thought about State affairs, made decisions, proclaimed decrees and orders that I never had the time to register but that were applied irrevocably; I also inspected my stock, my secondary caves, my emergency fortifications, my ramparts and watchtowers . . . ; I went everywhere, I checked everything; no theft, no ransacking, no intrusion, and nothing had moved; an unusual calm prevailed over the island; it grew stronger and stronger, in a stasis that ended up troubling me much more than its usual hostility;

I hesitated over the desire to pillage everything so as not to reveal to the savages the fact that this place was under control; it was reasonable; to destroy everything would set me back fifteen years back; to touch nothing out of weakness, vanity, or pride condemned me to death; the alternative tormented me over long days; I eventually left everything as it was, first because it had cost me so much that destroying it would have ruined my mental state; second, because another fact turned out to be just as decisive; examining my command with fresh eyes, I had realized that it was hardly distinguishable from nature's hysteria; the island made everything grow, everywhere, in all shapes and sizes, with chaos and disorder, as well as in unexpected harmony, sudden symmetries, constant collapses and rigid verticalities; the excessiveness stood alongside quiet equilibrium, the pillaging disturbed nothing but immense stability and order that was nothing but ordinary; the variation was so diverse and rapid, that my arrogant administration inserted itself without fantastic interruption or particular invention within an ever unpredictable system; this troubled me somewhat—so many years, yet so few things!—but it reassured me concerning the peril of savages;

*

I found the courage to return to where the footprint was; there, under the cover of seagrapes, I spent a few days observing the beach, trying to perceive movement other than the crustaceans, the stink bugs, and the turtles; I saw pairs of yellow snakes chase away the octopuses from under the almond trees; I saw processions of sperm whales escorted by thousands of dolphins, I saw fishing birds go back and forth between their lookout cays and the foam teeming with fish, and small-winged ones that fed by pecking at the sand; I saw the heat change the harbor into a glassy grease whereas the coastal leaves grew metallic; I saw soft waves make landfall on the sand with a sigh, and others as intense as molten salt, and whose holds cluttered with pebbles that mimicked the sound of frying as they unrolled; I saw reddish kelp emerge, harden, and vanish like ghosts in the brilliance of the shore; I saw sand so bright it was unbearable, or fade into a greyish coat that only the business of digging for seashells brought back to life . . . ; I saw many things time and time again, but nothing that had not already been inscribed into this soulless eternity that I had confronted for over twenty years;

I had to convince myself that I had not dreamed; that the footprint was indeed here; huddled under a few vetiver leaves, I left the seagrape tree and I advanced into the open, inch by inch, observing for long periods in a total steadiness; in this way, I felt capable of thwarting the vigilance of a few sentries positioned in the surroundings; at the precise location, the footprint was indeed there;

no longer was it a dense mass; it seemed soft, sensual, trembling, probably owing to the spurt of foam that had just reached it; I looked at it wide-eyed; it was heading toward the island's interior; the positioning painted the picture of a hasty landing; the only thing around for a thousand inches; no trace of a boat stem; no strikes of a pole or oar; I imagined a small boat swirling before being tossed sideways into the sand; I imagined its occupant leaping onto dry land to secure it, before pulling it under the muddle of trees; I felt (for just a moment) the desire to calculate the trajectory that the footprint indicated to find this hideout, but it was impossible for me to be detached from this human shape; it filled me with contradictory feelings; I had spent a good portion of my eternity protecting myself against all intrusion; first against that of the savages, and then by extension, and without realizing, against all existence that would not be a natural element of this island; I understood over time, by way of fear, then by way of loneliness, that any human form had been relegated to the back of my mind; and not only the shape of a foot but also a hand, a finger, a shoulder, a nose, a smile . . . a face . . . ; a wave of panic washed over me, and once again I found myself scurrying off to the cover of the olive trees;

*

back in my fortified cave, I began preparing my battle stations for invasion; I had been developing them for so long that they had succumbed to oblivion; it is true that the Department of War had fallen into disuse; it had been ages since I last wore any military decorations: admiral, artillery officer, commander of infantrymen, secretary of state of logistic affairs; sharpened by fear, my warrior tendencies returned very quickly; I cleared the arrow slits in the fence that climbing plants had blocked; I positioned the shooting stools; I aimed on the three-legged fiddlewood stools a series of muskets that I packed with powder and shots; I did likewise in other fortified sites spread over the surrounding area; numerous were my small, backup forts (strengthened with large shells and sharp bamboo); I had allocated them to different areas optimally using natural obstacles; the mangroves had offered me their knots of white branches and the suctioning mud of its swamps; directly above the fields— where I had planted tobacco, coffee, tomatoes, mysterious flowers, and which sometimes served as a holiday destination—the small, steep hills afforded me the advantage of height and a bird's-eye view over my potential enemy; I had concealed artillery platforms in gigantic trees, built into the shaded tree forks, and I had stored dry goods there, powder, and a comforting array of cold weapons; in case of invasion, I could therefore move in any direction, in complete safety, have retreats at my disposal, and harry my enemy as I pleased, impeding his ability to foresee my attacks; today, the situation was different; the landing had happened; the enemy was already patrolling the island; I abandoned the invasion operation procedures; I devoted myself to secondary fortifications, intended to withstand a siege or an extended invasion; I spent almost three moons going up and down, left and right, strengthening this, sealing that, removing termites, ants, snakes, millipedes, and spiders; in my cave, I retrieved the three powder kegs that I had secured in the driest spot; I opened them to distribute a good portion into each calabash that I carried to every fortification; finally, I tossed a hundred cups of powder in the bottom of an old barrel, armed with a long tow line; I was determined to blow everything up if these savages had the sacrilegious audacity to penetrate my sanctuary;

throughout this incessant fortification, I forgot about myself, and I forgot about the island; I felt light, freed of my usual rigidity; I no longer heard the obsessive splish-splash of the ten thousand clepsydras I had used for marking various places; I roamed free from rule, subjugated only to what my war mind dictated to me; such a frenzy dislodged me from a kind of mental and physical stiffness; it plunged me into such a revival of bodily gestures that it fatigued me very quickly; at night, I sank into my muggy alcove, deep down in my cave, surrounded by pistols and knives as sharp as a butcher's hook; I thus festered in a horrendous weariness that did not provide me with an ounce of rest; I was but a fever struck by the fear of losing everything, the yearning for war and the desire to kill; I perceived the irony of experiencing such an imagined situation, for so long and in vain, and which fell upon me at the highest degree of improbability; in this different way of watching, listening, and hearing, the island around me became flat, warm, and neutral so to speak; what remained hostile was confined to this intrusion filled to the extreme with its radiance, shadows, remoteness, and secret depths; the island was much more recalcitrant when I attempted to guess where the intruder and its accomplices were, and from which side it would launch its attack;

for a long time, I deemed it safer not to venture farther than the main fortress; I made sure to have an escape route, between the back of my fence and the entrance of my cave; I placed a few bundles of food, powder, and two more pistols; the idea was to run away well equipped in case of overwhelming hostile forces; then, I settled into the bartizan that overlooked the whole area, which afforded me a 360-degree view of the horizon 300 feet out; opposite me stood an impenetrable wall of trees that bordered a clearing; I had regularly weeded the parade ground around my dwelling, which gave me a surveillance perimeter of about 200 feet, nothing could venture upon it without being exposed; I installed my favorite musket, ready to fire, the canon was firmly in place, the butt wedged against my shoulder, my spy glass within quick reach, a few bags of spring water and a small drum of cassava, and I scrutinized the surroundings while waiting;

everything remained calm, motionless, and absent; trees were quivering as usual under the madness of Greater Antillean grackles, rats scrambling, plovers or wild ducks flying; the shudders of dry branches signaled a snake's racing away; bees flying and butterflies dancing in and out of sight in rays of sunlight, invisible until now; the tangled, trickling vines served as torturous vertebrae whereby lizards could escape; I counted the big, grumbling trees over and over, kept track of the light filtering through the mass of foliage . . . ; between the mossy trunks, I imagined my tuber, yam, and Napa cabbage gardens, probably ripe for harvest; in certain spots, I could see the sun, filtering through the foliage and reaching the ground in a puddle of bright gold; from time to time, the steam of a dormant soul, trapped in one of these beams, was revealed to me in a luminous divination that stirred my imagination; the strangest part was that I could perceive nothing threatening or frightening about this environment; this perception of an antagonistic power had nevertheless persecuted my everyday life for the past twenty years; now, nothing; nothing but a novel neutrality as a vast backdrop impacted by this intruder and his crew . . . ;

days and weeks, probably some seasons, passed by this way; I only left my position to look after my livestock, bring them grain, dry fruits, water, fodder, taken from my supplies; when my provisions ran out, I opened the parks, holding cells, pens, and pastures, so that they could get through without making a fuss; I watched over select fields: potato, wheat, barley, and company, in an endless war against the rats, ants, termites, birds . . . ; the rest of the time, I was stationed in the bartizan; motionless, focused, finger ready to pull on the trigger; I was patiently awaiting and observing everything around me; my neglected flag was now no more than a rag that even the trade wind could not revive; my notices, banners, signs, and announcements hid beneath the moss; the hedges were no longer even, and many pipes leaked a good amount of water; filled with a sort of detachment, I had become a fragment of my old self; no trouble, no turmoil, emulsified my body or my mind; I was plunged into a war against this intruder; an unmoving, yet violent, yet constant, yet total war; this aggressiveness was a great benefit to me; any aggressiveness is beneficial; it drains from a dark resolution deep down that sustains its survival; its power renders the rest secondary; it was what had allowed me to persevere in the face of this island, and to endure my long despair; it was now at its height, like a sun gone dark, and that shines as such; I would wait; I would wait for this other in order to fight him; I would wait to kill him, and to stay alive; but nothing moved or changed around there;

*

gripped by new doubt, I left my perch and ventured toward that wretched beach once more; there, I returned to the footprint with much less precaution, and I examined it to convince myself of its existence; there it was; this time it was dry; a jellyfish had washed up on it; baked time and again in the sun, the gelatinous mass had melted and filled the footprint with a gleaming oil that I had trouble looking at; my anxiety resurfaced intact at the first sight of this shape; it slid me into a wild fear; once again, I distanced myself in a sudden scare, as if it were the devil himself, without even getting back up, dragging my bottom across the ground and sweeping my arms to paddle the sand; when I reached the shade of seagrape trees, I began to run, bellowing in an inexplicable despair; immediately after, I returned to my watch in the bartizan; forefinger on the trigger, grip on the shoulder, I calmed down, and strictly readied myself for war; suppressing myself from making noise; limiting my movement, dividing my rest over short breaks; avoiding fire or releasing the slightest smell of grilled meat; I had cultivated the task of talking to myself, I had to continue doing it quietly, but I so dwelled on the same anxiety—imagining the cannibals and their long faces, stuffed—that I could only articulate a senseless gurgling to say the least but it engaged both my tongue and my

throat, and the useful resonance in my sinuses and chest; this
steady vibration in my bones formed a base of support;

months and months thus passed by, maybe less, maybe more; I
no longer kept track of moons and seasons, but I had ended up
incorporating a certain sense of time in its evolutions, and I felt
free to evaluate it instinctively; my perception shouted that lots
of time had passed by; my body had become somewhat numb;
my hands no longer trembled; my sleep was short and peaceful;
the crawling vines had invaded everything around me, swallowing my signs, desecrating my tracks and paths, climbing my
hedges and fences; my livestock was practically wild again even
though certain individuals continued to follow me closely, or
to gather in the old pastureland; my foundation exuded an old
state of neglect, but this insidious degradation did not bother
me; it was valuable that the intruder had no clue that some sort
of authority existed in this place;

*

I was going in circles; my vigilance blunted only to reappear
illogically and throw me into a steady panic for two or three
days; then it disappeared and reappeared once again; but most
often, I had the possibility of averting my eyes from the surroundings, and contemplating myself; my reason took over a bit
and made me realize I was only on the defensive; I was waiting
for the intruder, who had to be there somewhere watching out
for me as well, or maybe farther, settled in a peaceful field, living
the good life; I was no longer able to picture him as a worried
discoverer parting the sharp undergrowth; what he afforded me
was *a possessive authority;* he had settled in; he was taking possession of my island in some remote area; he relished my fruits,
and stuck flowers in his hair; he stored the water from my most
beautiful spring in awful containers; he chopped up wild pigs
that he would smoke before shoving them into clay jars likely
to roll toward the beach; the possibility that he was with others
died on its own, a horde would have never been able to be so
discreet, nor even a small group of primitives; he was alone, it

was paradoxically his strength; he could consequently be every-where, move faster, go farther, appear suddenly from anywhere, remain invisible for a long time; this obsession modified the re-lationship I maintained with this island; while I had spent these last twenty years keeping it at a distance, keeping it at bay so to speak, I started to better accept being within it, belonging to it, and that it was within me; the mere idea that I would lose it— the puerility of human nature!—made it desirable and precious; I then made the decision to no longer surrender the dominion of my kingdom; the intruder was in my house, and it was I who had to track him; find him and kill him;

*

I began to explore my island once again, perhaps with the fever that inhabited me at the time of my first investigations; at that time, I was concerned with moving fast, of getting an overall idea of the situation, of evaluating it as quickly as possible in order to make my decisions; this hunt was fueled by the same state of mind, going fast, finding fast, striking down the intruder fast in order to stay alive; the fear was just as strong, but it was no longer inspired by an unknown land: he was unknown, un-definable, and unlocatable; since he was nowhere, he was there-fore everywhere; all that constituted this island was inscribed strongly in the wake of his existence, and in the frightening suspense of a sudden appearance; it was useless to weigh myself down with water, food, and luggage; the island was demarcated by my influence; my vision of the island included useful logistics that allowed me to find shelter, a defensive perimeter, and food and drink anywhere; I got going when the birds sang before daybreak, those that foretell from the attributes of the light, and that, in my tense mind, constituted an auspicious moment; I led the exploration methodically; from what I thought was the most central point, I made gradually winding circles; these spirals allowed me to rake everything in with my eyes, nose, and ears; my back straightened, finger on the trigger; each shady spot hid him; each sway of the leaves betrayed him; the slightest scurry of a bug was a sign he was there, that he had seen me and

he would strike; from circle to circle, this alert subsided; from
then on, I was able to use Reason and explain to myself that he
did not expect me to be on the island, and definitely not that I
was looking for him; I had therefore a decisive advantage that
allowed me to relax and better track him;

each one of my spirals showed disparities in the landscape
which came simultaneously from the North and South, East
and West; I was surprised by this incredible variety of microclimates in such a tiny space; I crossed bushy fields, sparkling
with buds and bees, and glassy heat waves that produced blurry
ghosts on either side of my path; I had to make my way through
the mangroves, populated with thin and tortuous botanical
widow birds washing their feet in cloudy water; concretions
of oysters warped the roots of those mangrove trees making
them seem like toes with rheumatic fever afflicted with long
nails; clusters of hairy crabs in the midst of fornication clung
to the lower branches, creating big, pimply, breast-like forma-
tions; large fish napped in tree hollows, deep under the muddy
water, teeming with lots of things . . . ; I explored diaphanous
clearings, full of shrubs loaded with fruits, and where the air
so peacefully commanded the desire to sit . . . ; I crossed rocky
deserts whose stubborn intent was to petrify everything in some
sort of quartz, so much that my feet started to harden upon
mere contact with the gravel; I walked into thick spiderwebs,
bigger than my fist, and a thousand species of little lizards that
bellowed like cows . . . ; I surveyed fields of slender sprouts veg-
etating in the grip of big trees turned grey by sorrow; they rose
so wide, like giant barrels, and led to the top an exchange of
lively sparkles and scents, vines of light filtered through them by
the hundreds, yet they dispersed before reaching the darkness of
the ground . . . ; I saw assembling arborescent ferns growing in
a milt of thin water . . . ; I saw all sorts of landscapes, all sorts
of smelly shadows, all sorts of places stricken with great heat,
sharp salt or unbearable transparence; I even thought I caught
sight of a group of elves and dwarves in the flow of the river,
but these appearances were so gauzy that all I could do was
suspect them, as they were only visible when I looked carefully

in the right light; the result of which was never knowing if I had visions or if this island slipped into tales and wonders; it was without a doubt the strangest part: a different reality presented itself in a new enchantment that triggered in me a forgotten innocence;

I slept in all sorts of places, except of course in trees; I awoke surrounded by palaces of green, of mineral basilicas sanctified by dew; every morning was often a quivering wonder by dint of butterflies, flowers, and light that played with the wind; I would rest under curtains of epiphytic plants that coated the trees; in certain places my dreams were enchanted with giggling springs; sometimes, I met silences so powerful that they effaced the land-scape, leaving me only the attentive astonishment of my ear;

once, I thought I had detected movement; I threw myself to the ground, and I started to crawl up a slope carpeted with flowery grass; I reached the top of the incline which revealed a part of the island, and a piece of the horizon where the sea emerged; it was a giant gully; originating from the peaks, it descended sharply toward the shore; at each altitude, different types of trees had populated it, I could only see its extremities: a dome of leaf mass that exploded into millions of insects and just as many multicolored birds; a vapor escaped from it to stand still a few inches away and to begin knitting a variegation of mists; it was breathtaking; this landscape arose from something beyond the realm of existence;

another time, overhearing the noise of something fleeing in dis-tress, I crawled to the edges of a narrow hole; it was located at the base of a huge tree which seemed to rise from seven centu-ries of sadness; covered with flies and stink bugs, it exhaled a smell of antimony; I kept a close eye on the small, dark opening, expecting to see the intruder emerge, then I drew near to glance over it; the opening was barely usable; with a thousand precau-tions, I stuck my head in, then my shoulders, and then a part of my body; a large hollow appeared under the base of the tree; something had dug under the trellis of bulbs, leaving a gap of several feet; the roots had continued their descent toward the ground, assembling a weave of whitish rootlets in the air that formed an astounding, organic curiosity; it looked like nothing on earth, neither a vault, nor a crypt; it was a singular reality, outside of time, outside of the world; it seemed to live off an underground melancholia and from a lactescence that remembered the brilliant light from outside; I remained bewitched by what I saw there;

*

these minor discoveries contributed to each other; I maintained a vague confusion, some flashes of astonishment; for the rest, I did not give way to these outpourings, not because I was tracking this intruder and my mind stayed focused on this sole objective; the reason was different: *a tremendous sadness had arisen within me;* it had settled like a subtle grief and now inhabited me entirely; I felt it early on, incapable of identifying it, before it spread to my consciousness by thinking about it, I was able to then express it like this: there was an intruder on my island, and this intrusion—this other that for so many years had become an unthinkable notion—hurled me to the margins of this world like an obsolete thing; I who, after twenty years, positioned myself at the center of everything, on the very principle of completing this place, I felt as though I had become old, dusty, worn out, hung up, cut off from everything, and motionless within myself;

this feeling grew through my rediscovery of the island, stopping at each detail, tasting the air; it no longer had anything to do with the hostile block it used to be till then; I now perceived it like a mess of effervescence; the intruder was everywhere, invisible, nevertheless very intense; he was the one who gave shape to these landscapes, these butterflies, these scents, these enchanting lights; it affected and infected the whole down to its smallest parts; how I pictured him was the exact opposite from the little I perceived of myself; I imagined him quick, fast, free, leading a bohemian lifestyle on his narrow pirogue and navigating for ages with the joy of primitives; in any case, he knew how to come in and out of this hell that had detained me for twenty years now; the island was known to him; he knew where to go, and how to get there; nowhere had I perceived any inopportune disturbances, felled trees, squandered fruits, or ransacking caused by outsiders who come for supplies on this desert island; he, devoted himself to a precise mission, and with such accuracy that it did not disrupt the place whatsoever; this breeze of novelty swept my consciousness up like a blazing cyclone; at night, I lamented over this relic I had become; my imagination depicted the intruder as this being that sparkled with the desires that had long since withered inside me;

＊

I had lived in an unmoving world, replete with objects from a thousand-year-old frigate, forged from a dead past, ruminating endlessly, reliving that which had been; he, the invisible one, who came from naught and resembled nothing, established himself as pure novelty;

＊

this past that had immobilized me was fracturing inside; while I went from spiral to spiral on every part of this island, I had withdrawn into a painful relationship with myself; after two complete walks around my strange prison, I ended up sitting, astounded by exhaustion, on the final tip of the final headland; flocks of seabirds danced farandoles; their droppings rained down on the cliffs chiseled by salt and wind; I barely saw them; all I could see was the intruder, probably looking at them from somewhere else; I brooded over the feeling that he permeated the place; even the sky, even the sea, empty at all times for me, now highlighted his imperial eruption;

＊

I felt the pressing need to examine the footprint anew; it might have never existed; its absence would be unhoped for and would return me to my former splendor; I ran toward it on this cursed beach, I then had a vivid sensation: *it had disappeared, was no longer there, I had been mistaken!* . . . ; I was going to shout for joy when it suddenly reappeared, in the exact same place, beyond the reach of the swell;

once again, I fell to my knees before it, I began to go mad staring at it, my eyes drowning; I toppled over on my back in a sort of surrender to fate; then, I sang some obscure song, springing from a crypt in my mind; I recognized it, I recognized it not; a verse about a sailor, a harbor, and a binge; familiar melody; I was undoubtedly a sailor . . . ; these strange memories came back in dribs and drabs; in twenty years, just as many things came to mind as I had brought back from the boat: words from weird languages . . . a taste for hats and bracelets . . . the adroitness with a compass and triangle . . . the multipurpose dexterity of my hands . . . my skill at fortifications . . . my science for machinery to collect water, use the wind, transport heavy things . . . my ingenuity to grow fruit plants from a cutting, to sow and harvest despite the fury of the rats . . . ; I never felt like I had any sort of expertise, always a pleasant surprise to see my hands excel in work; a virtuosity lay deep within my obscure memory; it sprang from misplaced boxes in my mind; boxes forgotten, that opened without any reason, closed without a sound, and left me flabbergasted; this Sapiens, I was convinced, made me an unordinary human being; I must have been very important, an engineer of a certain science, a structural engineer, or plantation master, or naval captain; my memory had gone away, but my aptitude to subdue misfortune had remained intact; it must certainly be this *enigmatic experience,* undefined, unlimited, that I celebrated unknowingly within me; that equally I searched for, and that I had deployed with as much vanity in the face of this prison-island . . . ; over these twenty years, I had looked deeper within myself, seeking my limits, my lost powers, and all the reasons for which divinities had picked me to confront the power of this island; I sang;

*

I do not know how long I lay on my back next to the footprint, letting myself be rocked by strange whims, experiencing frenzies I thought I had overcome and which came back to me now, in a thousand chaotic illusions; I sang, I bellowed, I rambled aloud; I insulted myself and insulted the intruder as well when I felt like he was looking at me from behind a cloud, or that he was sneaking in right behind a large turtle in the throes of laying season; I no longer wanted to leave the footprint, watching it at all times, no longer examining it but instead each glance was a real blow to my awareness;

*

I probably stayed on this beach for many a season; as close as possible to the footprint; protecting it from the brutality of the foam; building it a small hut for fear that the heat of the sun would make it go away; waking up there, next to it; washing up there, next to it; fishing next to it; gulping down a bunch of grapes, lying there, next to it; the footprint changed every day to the rhythm of the beach which was also no longer the same: there were good reasons to be fascinated with this bizarre permanence of the sand, entirely conceived of fluidity, difference, and change; the footprint, as for it, was not to be outdone; while being stared at, it transformed before my feverish eyes into a face without features: that of the intruder; in a hallucinatory turn, it suddenly became a voice; if not, it was erected as a sign that the intruder had left in my place: a warning, or a call, a boundary marker or a symbol of possession; sometimes it screamed at me: *I have come!* . . . and other times: *I am here, and here to stay!* . . . ; or, it began to express the simple desire that the intruder had to stretch his legs, inflicting a kick into the sand with his whole foot;

I began to imagine him in detail; he must have been very tall, very heavy, half giant, considering the impact that the footprint formed; my memory released zones of twilight, and I saw him with a negro posture, or Indian in the way he painted his face with ground achiote; anyway, he was one of these hideous descendants of the sun, used to being tanned by the salt, who knew how to read the stars and control the wind with his nostrils alone; he must have known this region well, to roam it fearlessly in long solitude; his pirogue must have been large enough to hold up so long on the high seas; where had he hidden it? . . . in which unknown cove? . . . had his accomplices just dropped him off and were they to come back to get him one of these days? . . . who was he to be so dexterous, to manage to arrive here, and to remain unnoticed? . . . this art made him a warrior capable of destroying me in no time at all; thousands of atrocious weapons came to mind, they must have been across his shoulders, beating against his shoulder blades, burdening his hips; *studded ax; sharp clubs; rippers' javelins; poison darts; whalebone knives; seashell-tipped war club* . . . ; he must have been naked, with just a sheath for his Minotaur penis; his hair must have been braided with lizard blood; and his ears pierced with stems of jade stamped with malachite; and his forehead scrunched so flat and ugly allowing him to see both the ground and the sky . . . ;

he was formed and deformed with insane images that filled my head; at times, he appeared blue with yellowish eyes; other times, covered in a slurry of plants like a living thorn bush; or with rings jingling from his nostrils, lips, and ears, while tattoos transformed his skin into an exterior of evil spells . . . ; he continually changed in a frenzy, suddenly emerging as a bearded redhead, with a steel hook for a right hand, Portuguese, Spanish, or English, maybe one of those Frenchmen who believe themselves to be the rulers of little islands . . . ; but these assumptions did not last long; it was impossible for him to take part in this world that the frigate had imposed upon me; it was an other, like this island, in an irreversible strangeness;

I began to imagine him with slanted eyes, or covered by a turban, his head enclosed in a pickelhaube helmet while displaying a Turkish saber and riding a camel; I saw him among his people in the midst of dark and mysterious ceremonies where he drank juices from stones and read prophecies spread across the stars; I saw him worship feathers and claim to be from a saurian family next to imperturbable rivers ... ; he must have carried away the intestines of his relatives in the large shell of a funeral urn, which allowed him to talk to whatever evil was in the sky; he must have grilled red corn when his wives gave birth or ordered it to rain handfuls of pollen ... ; I knew well that it was only feverish illusions, but I loved, I must confess, to stimulate them to excess, to dwell upon them endlessly, vaguely enjoying these childish illusions that filled me with a surge of existence, unknown to my being for the past two decades;

the more I imagined him in primitive forms—especially the most grotesque—the better I felt to no longer be part of the humanity that had forgotten me, and that I had forgotten; I was somewhere else, *in the void of the outside,* and I looked at it screaming in vain; neither he nor anyone heard me; I was part of this thing that was the island, buried within it, and he was the human one; he came from the horizon, he rode on the winds, he was able to leave again; he did not need me, yet I was nothing without him; the prison-island was but a twig in his vast universe, for me on the contrary it was really everything, my beginning, my present, and my end, my whole past and my whole future ... ; through a slow alchemy, unaware of it, I renounced my fears and started to consider him differently; he thus had in his possession something I did not, something so infinite which I had squandered in my desire to protect it: he was *the entire elsewhere, the entire possible* as well;

suddenly, while observing the footprint, I realized it came from a right foot; this was a good omen, the left would have brought nothing good; it was said that in some slave tribes, they made sure visitors entered the kingdom on their right foot; that there were, in seven parts of the world, stairs where the number of steps were calculated to ensure that the last footstep, the one that reached the temple, was with the right foot ... ; that certain apostles of Christ left only the imprint of their right foot

in the dust, and that the mothers of these great prophets moved
only in their right toes while sleeping . . . ; so, despite the ridicu-
lousness of these superstitions, the footprint no longer seemed
hostile; *it belonged to someone that fate had led to me;* it answered to years of terror and calling out before the deserted
horizon; he was every bit as legitimate as I was on this island,
perhaps just as confused as I was in the beginning; I smiled at
the idea of him trembling with fear atop a tree; I imagined the
face of surprise he would make upon discovering me before
him; I had no idea how he pictured me; if he were aware of this
splendor I thought I embodied until then . . . ; he might have
seen me pass and believed he was seeing an archangel of hell,
and from that moment he hid away in a pig burrow; I toyed
with the idea that he was the only survivor of an event as mysterious as the one that had thrown me here, and that together we
could achieve civilization on the island; to subjugate it to what
we had best inside of this human condition from which we ultimately carried the burden; and then: *what did I have to lose?*
twenty years of solitude! . . . ; *what harm could he do?* to thrust
me somehow out of this fixed oubliette! . . . ; the idea that I had
once wanted to kill him frightened me, or that I had imagined
he could be after my hide; if this fear was still present, it was
effortlessly heightened by the elation that suddenly inhabited
me; *I wanted to meet him, to trust him, and to do everything in
my power so that he trusted me;* and should the worst occur—if
he killed me, mutilated me, reduced me to slavery—I would
let him because he would still have offered me a moment of
contact, touch, encounter, that nothing could ever really alter;
a moment undoubtedly short but which would remain for me
a spectacular second—one during which, after twenty years of
involution, I would live again;

*

my fingers fumbling, I tried to find a face under the pile of hair
and beard where my hat had left my eyes free; with my sharpest
knife, I started to trim everything, shave everything, including
my head and my face, even the hair on my arms and my chest

and my legs; I was dismayed upon seeing the mass of hair that spread around me; a veritable coat that I had not even noticed; something unusual, I entered the water to scrub myself, and scrub myself again; I wanted my human skin to appear, for it to be visible, I wanted for him to recognize myself in him; it was not an intruder, *it was an other;* an other who had a bit to do with this vacuity I had become; someone endlessly rich with everything that was not from here, who could return me to what I once had been; I packed fruits, I stacked cassavas along with mango and raspberry wine in a basket; I took some apple-vine jam for him, a dried boxfish, a ball of royal jelly . . . tiny wonders with which I brightened up my everyday life in hell; and ballasted with all these offerings, I set off once more to look for him . . . ;

Captain's Log

July 30—In the year of our Lord 1659—Yesterday, we also lost a man due to scurvy. The surgeon refused to keep him on board. I had him sewn very quickly in a shroud of hessian. We gathered to pray for the dead. The ceremony was much slower than usual. Perhaps because of the very place where we sailed: the blue algae had been fading for a long time under a carpet of jellyfish. The body tipped over in this living, gelatinous mass, as if these thousands of creatures by their sole throng had created a huge monster that kept an eye out for the ship. The cadaver of the unfortunate man had trouble sinking, but the twelve-pound balls eventually pulled him to the bottom, nevertheless with a disturbing slowness. He was able to disappear into the abyss and hand his soul over to God. I dare not write it, but may the divinities that animate these jellyfish protect him just as much . . .

August 5—In the year of our Lord 1659—We are getting closer to the mainland. After the sandbanks and the coral hamlets, the first islands were spotted. These are always pleasant things to see. They were announced by the smell of spices, the mists from vegetation, and birds taking flight that no longer needed to rest on our yardarms. It is always a miracle to see one cut through an empty horizon, as if it came from the abyss. Each time it prompts the same satisfaction, especially because we benefit from filling the barrels with spring water, collecting two or three manatees or wild pigs to smoke as they do in the wild. It is a nice change from the wormy, salted meat and dry, leathery biscuits.

*August 17—In the year of our Lord 1659—*This morning, while leaving an unknown little island where we had berthed for a few days, I thought about heading to an old passage where I had sailed a very long time ago. Something had begun to knock around my head and piqued my memory and curiosity a bit . . . The sailing master is not happy. Where we are heading, the charts are unpredictable. To reassure him, I increased the soundings and doubled the lookout posts . . .

2

THE SMALL PERSON

it is difficult to describe the elation that carried my mind away; my stride was swift and my back relaxed; I got rid of my old animal-skin rags to free my arms; I was wearing just this livery that protected my knees against the thorns; a loose-fitting top covered my shoulder and exposed my chest and belly; I wanted him to see my arms and legs, the movement of my respiration, the whole of my body; my eyes themselves had joined the party, and tried to express a part of my soul; I had come out of the deepest pit yearning to hoist myself to the window of my pupils; I had even left behind the straps that had been wrapped around my feet for some time; I went barefoot so the invisible other could see my toes; as a result, I could sense the island's entire existence beneath my naked heels; the soft, dense grasses; the suction of mud and bogs; the dry heat on the rocky ground . . .

I often slipped because I had left my rudimentary walking stick behind; it was pleasant to abandon all sepulchral rigidity in the way I walked, I turned, I sat, to simply be alive . . . ; this time, I moved exposed, making as much noise as possible with my words, songs, long exclamations, and my calls every hundred feet; I shouted: *Holà holà, where are you, my little fellow?* . . . and I went on like this, ready to see him pop out of a big tree, or emerge from the darkness of a bamboo gully;

there was so much disorder in my wandering that it sent the birds flying; they sprang from everywhere, in a compact flock that went wild in every direction and then reassembled right in the face of danger; the bushes shook under frenetic flights, probably from fowl nesting on the ground, but also from rats, snakes, or those wretched cats who had escaped from the frigate

and not stopped proliferating since; I had combatted this problem by hunting and eating them; I made recorders with their
bones; I hung their skulls above the sowing to scare the Greater
Antillean grackles away; I also used them for live bait to catch
sharks, to make oil from their livers or the delicacy of shark fin
soup; I was happy to be noisy; I had always crept between the
hostilities of this place, with careful steps, with anxious steps,
then with steps so stiff that they were confined in a silent contri-
tion; now, this slovenliness was finally ridding me of a thousand
years of numbness;

it was impossible to measure the distance I traveled each day; I
walked to the point of exhaustion, stopping only to hunt a cat,
or a young bird, and to cook it with pomp and circumstance;
I wanted the aroma of grilled flesh to spread in every direction
and for this bugger to come running; I made cat, but also rabbit, but also turtledoves and ortolans; I cooked a large lizard
that reminded me of bison meat which I stuffed with quail eggs;
I even cooked a water snake that had jumped on me during
my bath; the big new thing was bathing; approaching rivers
was accompanied by the desire to dive in, to wash, to detach
the thousand-year-old grime that covered me all over, and that
flaked away little by little; these fresh waters seemed so engaging to me that I lay down in there for a very long time without
moving; then hundreds of crawfish rushed around me, allowing
me to grab them by the handful and make nice fricassees in my
iron bowl; incidentally, when I was cooking them I made an ap-
palling discovery to say the least; I had squatted down next to
my little fire, delighted with the crackling of the crawfish in my
coconut oil, when I discovered my toenails; my heart clenched;
I thought I saw an animal paw, equipped with glassy, long, and
deformed claws; over these twenty years my nails had grown
wildly, giving me bear paws to which I had never really paid any
attention; the sight of my hands was even sadder; the nails were
cut, broken, striated, cracked, they curved almost like talons
and of different lengths; I started to meticulously shorten them
all, then to scrub them with my knife, until I had rendered my
fingernails and toenails suitable once more;

unfortunately, this was not the only dismay; the next one concerned my illusions about my speech; apart from the songs,
I surveyed the undergrowth, the fields and the hills, well exposed to the four winds, and by shouting: *Holà!* . . . ; from each
headland—when the conditions allowed for my voice to carry
as far as possible—I yelled one word with all my might, one
verse of my little book, something that could notify this other
that a brother lived here and that he was looking for him; in my
mind, I was pronouncing one thing, but the surprise came all of
a sudden when I heard myself; I had first screamed: *Holà!* . . .
my mind was convinced, my reason had registered it as such;
but where I had shouted it—on the edge of a cliff, that overlooked the cliffs below—my voice had carried against the latter,
provoking a sort of echo that reverberated what I had screamed:
a vague grunt! . . . ; something that I barely recognized and that
did not match anything I thought I had articulated;

I almost fell backward; my heart beating, I uttered some words,
one or two sentences, I sang a few verses and two of my oldest
songs; each time, I only perceived whistling or grunting, bleat-
ing, hooting, cackling in return . . . sounds that brought me
closer to what constituted my universe of sound rather than
the composition of human speech; my words had degenerated
into frightening replicas of these animal calls that surrounded
me the entire time;

I could have cried about it, but my elation toward this other
was such that I was satisfied with my awareness of it; I remained facing these cliffs that reverberated the echo, and there,
for a beautiful eternity, at least for a few weeks, I verified that
the images of words in my mind matched the sounds that came
from my throat; I nearly gave up many times, fearing a fatal
deformation of my larynx, that I had lost the grace of speech;
but some things came back; the echo returned a few phonemes,
then syllables, finally words that constituted imitation of
phrases; I wandered once again toward my fellow human being,
continuing the laborious task of bringing back the blessing of
the word;

*

my lord, a mixture of dismay and elation inhabited me; I was afflicted with discovering what I had really become; nevertheless, the elation to meet this other, to get back in touch with my human side, filled with me joy; by isolating myself on the island, by isolating myself from the island, I had also been isolated from my own self; my life had simply adapted to what was functionally vital in this hostile power; I had been in decadent harmony with her; the island had inhaled me, maybe even digested, molded me as it pleased; doubting the aptness of my reasoning and of my senses, I began to question colors, flavors, or smells that I thought I had identified; one second did not go by without checking to see whether what I was perceiving at the time could be in accordance with what was possible in this place; it was then that I realized, for I don't know how long, that the sky was not blue to me; it did not have any color, it was a lid; it was a void; it was an abyss; what I perceived from it was only an illusion born from some sort of emotion; the same phenomenon occurred in regard to the sea, and by extension to the whole island; from then on, whenever I walked along a beach, I had to teach myself to look rationally again; I looked for the blues, the violets, the yellows, the reds, the grey tints of the clouds, the creamy whites, whitewashed or sparkling from the foam; in the leaves I discovered bright greens, light greens, warm greens, dark greens, greens leaning on the red or shaped by yellow; I did likewise for each flower, each animal, each object; in all of that, light conducted endless chromatic fluidities; I soon progressed toward an intoxicating explosion of incessant reflections, of splendid scintillations; I wandered in a palace of diamonds and fine gold glimmering in the radiance of a thousand torches; strangely enough, in front of a spectacle so consistent, so complete, I began to shiver; my legs lost their drive; everything was too new, too renewed, too amazing; everything appeared differently to me, in a clear abundance; my mind had become dizzyingly mobile; I often had to sit, to close my eyes to ward off this flood of information that asphyxiated me at times; to escape it, I fell asleep all at once, for a long time, the way newborns do to filter out the overwhelming world around them;

*

I needed time to adjust to my new state of mind, and to rediscover a relative serenity; the elation had left me; I was more sober, calmer, and more attentive to myself and to the details in my surroundings; I thanked the heavens for this unexpected and general rediscovery; without it, the other would have only met a clawed, grunting, agitated, hysterical beast; now, I strolled peacefully; before my eyes were only questions; my reasoning was a long list of doubts, weighing them; I regulated the sounds that came out of my mouth to confer on them the most humanity possible; and my heart, somewhat slowed down, handled the effervescence of smells and colors that accompanied my wanderings better; I continued in this way toward the other; and this is when I saw him;

there he was, right in front of me, standing stock-still in a field; he was chewing red berries that he may have picked from the surrounding shrubs; he must have been quite old; grey hair; dark and dull eyes; his jaw moved convulsively, but his air seemed one of the most haughty; he looked at me unsurprised but also without any friendship, only bothered to see me disturb his peace; after I greeted him as ceremoniously as possible, I began to slowly speak to him; he took two steps back, quivering; I halted, permeated by a soothing slowness; ensuring the elegance of my movements, I showed him one by one the delicacies I had for him; he remained expressionless; I sat in the field, and showed him how I savored a few of these delicious wonders I took out of my calabashes; at the same time, I arranged the rest in front of me, and with an affable gesture invited him to partake; he smelled so strongly that it overwhelmed the field and assaulted my nostrils; it was . . . ; *it was not unfamiliar . . .* ; suddenly, I was struck by a jolt of my mind; but there was so much wisdom in his eyes that I spoke to him once more; I told him what I thought I was and what I had experienced; I spoke about the island, the frigate, the rats, the cats, my fields, my beehives, my beached boat, my attempts to leave the island on bamboo and gum rafts . . . ; at a total loss; I kept giving details of many an event, until he stepped backward and started to move away; this is when I saw . . . the horns of a billy goat . . . and also when I started to bawl out of surprise and shame . . . ;

this old goat had looked much more human than I did . . . ; thinking I had gone crazy, I rushed toward the darkness of a gully where I curled up in despair; impossible to understand what had happened to me; such a hallucination was the sign of my mind crumbling; I needed several hours of deep thought to admit that this misfortune was but a strong desire for the other; an unquenchable thirst for a drop of humanity; moving once again, this machine of desires that I was able to identify allowed me to explore this place much better than at any other period of my solitary life; I did not move forward spatially: I surveyed small plenitudes and sudden emotional depths; each step was an opportunity for knowledge; each hilltop, an ever-wondrous place of learning; whatever human or sensitive things surrounded me—trees, bugs, leaves, rocks and moss, wind and cliffs—were revealed unto me; bursts of awareness, tenderness flowing; true moments of affection and melancholy; I spent my days of walking really looking at this existence; I was finally capable of feeling what we shared; just as I did, each of us did our best to live with what was provided; just as I did, each of us got by with our tricks to survive; they lived just as I did "into this outside," at the bottom of this dungeon, and became as such my fellow companions of misfortune, my brothers in perdition; we were in the same boat and in the same fatality; I was happy with that, and tormented as well;

*

my surprises were not over; I had sprinkled the island with a third line of defense: stockpile holes dug at the base of cliffs; they dated back to my daily fear of a savage invasion; I had named them—*Strategic Points, Tactical Flanks, Operational*

Camps, Support Base, Supplies and Resources . . .—in accordance with the vocabulary assembled from my memory lapses; they allowed me to take refuge anywhere on the island without missing the basics for a new post; in the course of my raucous excursions in search of this other, driven by old reflexes, I revisited these places one by one; all were concealed properly with bushes that made them impossible to detect; for the sake of civilizing this island, I routinely named these stockpiles with a sign discreetly placed in the nearby surroundings; each time I restocked, I refreshed the faded ink, or I covered them again with marks, words, or sentences taken from my dear little book; so, that day, I returned to one of these bases in a mineral hollow, concealed by fragrant bushes that intoxicated a swarm of red bees and hairy caterpillars; it was constituted of a fiddlewood hut, embedded in a pile of fallen rock; in front gurgled a river that cast its water onto the crackling pebbles; while searching for the placard that should have been there, I stumbled upon a piece of bark that displayed only a vile scribble; not only was this scrawl illegible, but it also indicated the hand of a maniac; the name of the place, the seal of my ascendancy, the mark of my splendor, was in fact but a soulless scrawling . . . ;

I ran away, like a chicken with its head chopped off, searching for the nearest placards, signs, and markers; and, each time, it was one bitter discovery after the other; a few of the signs still had words, *Yé, Tobacco, Congo, Odono, Jupiter, Niger, Nice Bridge* . . . ; a few others, the oldest ones, looked like what I had intended to write: *Way of the Word, Telling and Thinking, Conviction* . . . ; but the sun and rain had bleached the beginning of sentences on the others, and what I had written over it no longer made sense: combinations of syllables or letters that ran into each other with disheartening absurdity, KKKOP, IIIMBV, ILILILX . . . and so on . . .

rather than crying, I convinced myself I was happier this way; I took the time to wash each sign; first, I carefully erased what was next to the incantation; then, with all the care, politeness, awareness, will, and desire possible, I rewrote a description on them—*Escape . . . Immortal Coachman . . . Krisis . . . Variation . . . Immobile . . .*—praying to the Heavens that I had really written what I had meant to write . . .

*

the doubt about the overall quality of what I restored, or that I brought back from within myself, remained firmly healthy; I used it as embers of surveillance: to better observe myself, better watch myself, scrutinize the purpose of my gestures, listen to what I sang as something foreign to my mouth, keep an eye on my writing and reread the slightest markings a thousand times . . . ; this reaction was positive to my understanding; keeping my spirits up despite the assessment of all these regressions, I reacted as does a human, taking the matter into my own hands; for me, it seemed obvious that a solitary mind is first and foremost an abyss of illusions; knowing this made me feel like being lost in a raging sea holding onto this sole lifeline that was nothing more than my vital self, the remnants of my humanity . . .

I paid close attention to this resurrection that operated at the discretion of my wanderings; seeking this other threw me into productive changes; until then I had buried myself in a swamp of madness fermenting in the back of my head; since that time, I dedicated my forces to camp outside, in the open, vulnerable to passing showers and the sun; truly outdoors, as if on the edge of a cliff that was exposed to the fury of storms; I had always remained under the cover of tents, huts, caves, caverns, and gullies, I lived outdoors—*within* the outdoors, even; I ate outside, worked outside, slept outside, dreamed outside, peed and defecated outside; I ran from retreats, remaining highly exposed, to avoid being taken away by another evil spell; once again I began to rediscover everything; and it was not only this care and doubt that sharpened my nose, ears, eyes, or even my mouth, nor was it amplifying the palpation of my hands: it was mainly the impalpable and unclear *appearance without warning* of this other that fate had finally led to me; he escorted my steps; he created a thousand possibilities for each of my explorations in a new land; I imagined he had seen what I saw, in such a way that his gaze now preceded mine on top of what I observed; and not only did he precede it: he conditioned it; I attempted to feel what he had felt upon stumbling on a bunch of bird nests; if he had shivered in front of this old pig whose head was mysteriously covered with a yellowish mane . . . ; I sensed his existence, which gave me colors, which determined my own impressions; and on top of all of this, it was impossible for me not to imagine *his infinite desire of this place* after undoubted months of solitary navigation; he had begun to invest in it with such love that it made me jealous, which in return generated in me a burning covetousness for the entire island . . . ;

*

wandering kept bringing me back to my old grounds; although it felt as though I was purely roaming about, I always happened upon one of my old storehouses, or the perimeter of my barley, rice, coffee, wheat, or corn plantations . . . ; no matter what I did, I found myself at some point in the day right next to a stockpile of weapons or food; in fact, I did not wander in any particular way but remained intimately drawn to these places; I went back up to each space of this island that was familiar and, imperceptibly, I avoided all the others; to fight this mechanical action, I began to "reflect" on my movements; the simplest of which was to put myself in the other's shoes and to imagine myself castaway on this prison-like island, and organizing my exploration according to an emotion that must have been his; thus, I came out of the ruts of my mind, and I went outside, into the outside, exposed . . .

*

from this moment, something else oriented me without guiding me; a roving force; it steered my footsteps, but remained calmly outside of me; from time to time, it crossed my mind, aroused my desires, bestowed an unexpected impulse within me; I could unreasonably about-face, or begin to hurtle down a slope where creaking bamboo seemed to have called me; thus I crossed over areas invisible until then; a very strong feeling of oddness began to rise from the endless renewal of heavy rainforest or quivering wilderness . . .

I saw trunks with split bark that smelled of sulfur and bay rum tree; I crossed the muddy fields, bristling with jagged rocks, covered in signs that, in forgotten times, must have been used for feasts of savages . . .

I discovered lots of vines; they had invaded surrounding trees and shrubs, meshing over and over with every living thing around them, strangling it all; the vines were entangled in a muddle that I had to cut with my large saber; I thought I heard whining from everything that was caught in their vise; they threw a constellation of bright yellow flowers toward the sun, voracious for the light, that attracted flocks of hummingbirds and a number of small jumping monkeys;

I saw a silent landscape, or more exactly: its substance was made of silence; like a sudden hole that everything with noise and disturbance avoided at all cost; this place was covered with black stones, eroded by the sharpness of the wind; it was riddled with relatively steep craters where pieces of carbon dust lay, impossible to define, shining like stardust; the place must certainly have been bombarded by thousands of cannonballs that came from the depths of the sky; only the movements of termites that ate the pumice stone, and a number of green-hair spiders whose viscous traps decimated lizards and tiny bats could be seen . . .

in the dense undergrowth, certain extremely muggy shaded areas gave rise to geysers of emotions within me; they sent me back to a strange world; that of the boat with which I had rebuilt my life from peaceful sources, charming meadows, castles and cities, harbors and cobblestone lanes; the other world that arose in me in these humid shaded areas was constituted of reddish fields, shores opening onto rough seas, tributaries as immeasurable as larger rivers which in turn were similar to vast oceans; I discerned plant-covered paths where ferns with blue and golden reflections grew; plants that looked like little crowns circled around huge trunks whose tops were impossible to make out, or even to decide whether they were real trees . . . ; it filled me with emotion, like I was brought back to a childhood vault; I lingered so long in these seeping shaded areas that I populated them with elves, imps, korrigans, of which I had brought back images from the boat; I even thought I caught glimpses in blurry images of the shape of a castle whose donjon rose not unlike a resinous tree . . . but such associations could not last: these places were from a different reality than that of castles . . . ; those images brought back from the frigate inhabited my mind as much as they projected a defiant influence onto all the things that did not seem related to them . . .

*

while rediscovering the island, the impression that grew in my mind was one of "fierce thickness," a primordial state of which I perceived only a tiny bit, that cared little about my fortifications, pasturelands, and possessions; the island existed here as it always had—huge, endless—and I thought I had domesticated it; I felt infinitesimal in front of such profusion; it spread endlessly in front of my now clear gaze; and my eyes were not the only thing overwhelmed, it was also this whole order that I had implemented by means of a great deal of defiant rules and laws, and that, by being projected onto my surroundings, had now sunk within me; these proud ramparts fell one after the other under the intertwined explosion of each of my senses;

fragrant winds continued to wash over me; each place had its very own; blended by the wind while retaining their individual intensities; dozens of fragrances floated above a backwater, in line with the cassava branches, on sunny rocky grounds where citronella plants swayed; they blanketed the ground around the spotted bark trees, skin-soft spotted bark—and I crossed them while moving something invisible aside with chaotic arm movements, you'd think I was moving through curtains of tulle . . . ; unable to identify them, I held onto familiar aromas, olfactory similarities that reassured me by evoking roses, jasmine, papaya, plumeria, thyme, or violets . . . ; but at once I could perceive the shortfalls, to the extent that my mind began to exuberantly combine them; which produced deposits of heliotrope in the myrrh, circles of benzoin and oregano on burned sand, traces of almonds in camphor nets . . . ; thousands of absurd combinations that became concrete with tens of thousands of dashes—*ylang-ylang-jasmine-iris, anise-thyme-poop-tuberose-lemon, rosemary-plumeria-opoponax-stone-cold* . . .—while in my overwhelmed mind they aroused images of monasteries upholstered with golden leaves, cordage entangled in a water vortex, ashen cities crushed by the sun, or temples drooping into soft ruins in fields of lavender . . . ; in addition to that, thousands and thousands of senses, aborted memories, evaporative resurgences, besieged my awareness to stagnate for a while, and without any purpose;

*

when I escaped this exhilaration of scents, I was carried away by what I could hear; the island had always been noisy: the crashing of certain shores, the fury of the wind against the cliffs, leaves rustling, masses of birds calling, the crackling of thousands of bugs that filled the nights; in addition, there was the bacchanal of my pets, of rats in my crops, or of geckos that cursed the moon . . . without taking into account the cacophony of click-clack, splish-splash, gobble-gobble, bing, swish swish, zing zing, and cling zing, which altered the shadows with a touch of evil spell . . . ; this uproar had persecuted me for many years; to survive it, I had to stop trying to understand these hullabaloo plots, and, now that I think of it, I spent most of my time refusing to hear them; the gates of my mind, filtering the whole island, had rendered it almost voiceless and silent; what I kept hearing was: the sounds of birds that I was used to hunting, the whining of my pets when in need, the calm of the wind right before the storm; or even: the trembling of rocks when an earthquake began to emerge and running me out of the arches and caves; now—as if I had wanted to hear what this Other heard, as if I were jealous of the innocence of his ears—my hearing frolicked about with such strong desire; the sounds of my first years came back to me distortedly fluid and compact at the same time, where each element fueled an enormous wholeness with its unique touch;

the indistinct noise of birds evolved into chirping, whistling, tweeting, quacking, and quack-quack . . . ; they cackled, squawked, clucked, and cooed in a thousand and twelve ways, which drew my attention to egrets, colorful robins, weird beaks, the gleaming feathers, and to unusual ways of flying; springs whispered; rivers voiced joyful or sad melodies; the cliffs sounded like guitars; the vague hullabaloo throughout the day was transformed in a constellation that I could identify, and that spread as the orchestra ripples; it provided a different truth to lighted spaces, to dark places, to multiple altitudes or clearings; a real resounding sculpture that allowed me to perceive the movement of time and the densities of different places that transformed according to this movement . . . ;

*

ever since I was convinced that this Other was here, and that he lived here with such intensity, I realized how frozen my space had remained; how I had maintained an immobility on this island as solid as it was basic; and how springs had only been useful, to the extent that they did not sing as they did today, overtly offering me the delicate nature of living water, and uterine shades that threw my mind and body into a panic . . . ;

*

just to be precise, my lord, when I thought about him, *about this Other,* I now put a capital letter on the word . . .

*

the wind blew a thousand different ways, with varying rhythms, branches, sands, and the flatness of the fields; it smashed into trunks, climbed the bark, the clattering at times causing a cascade of dead leaves that seemingly offered me meager applause; birds allowed me to see the wind's lines of action, they followed its ascending turns, dispersed when the wind started to skim the ground . . . ; bees and other flying things swarmed in the breeze as it spread across the land, like ripples growing in invisible water; the slightest plant fed from butterflies, transformed its flowers into hummingbirds, transmuted its leaves into groups of insects . . . a living instability that the wind intensified while increasing its quakes, leaps, and sudden flights;

*

the trees suddenly seemed alive; they connected in secret unions that I sometimes walked along in silence, I lowered my head so as not to disturb; I was all the more stunned that, since my arrival, I had only considered trees in order to assess their dangerous nature; all harbored poison with more or less fervor; to varying extents, all had been suspected of spreading fevers or old bewitchments; I had ranked them according to the level of anxiety I felt in front of them; on this basis, a good portion of time was devoted to naming them by using memories that sprang to mind or from the world the frigate had given me; I called them: *witch-oak, dragon-birch, snake-baobab tree, acid-willow* . . . based on resemblances and some vague analogies; I had also named all sorts of weird fruits, *apples, grapes, cherries, raspberries,* until I inevitably resorted to dashes in order to define an irreducible singularity—I then called them: *vine-apple, hill-apricot, beef-mango, dog-almond tree, seashore-grapes* . . . ; naming had undoubtedly been the proudest accomplishment of my mind; but here, now, in this maelstrom that this Other triggered, I found nothing to name, nor even how to name; I could no longer even consider naming; I could do little more than look, guess the streams of more or less benevolent *apparitions,* and be as one with them for better or worse; I felt as if I were before powers whose origins exceeded mine by thousands of years, and that undoubtedly would still be in this place many boundless centuries after me . . . ; I had become infinitesimal;

*

with these illusions in mind, I wandered along forgetting at times that I was searching for this Other that overwhelmed me so; I was intoxicated by discoveries and a lack of comprehension; in a troubled rapture, I was content to follow the scents, fragrances, music of the wind; I ended up turning back to simply smell, touch, see, or hear, astounded with this island that had remained outside my haughty management's reach; with my methods, regulations, and laws, my imagination and principles, over all these years, I had been but a negligible film over this density unable to figure it out; or perhaps I had figured out this island too much, which persuaded me to live within an illusion of an opera stage, and nebulous beliefs with weak foundations;

over these twenty years, my lord, I had faced this island, with the constant feeling of its threat; my efforts had consisted in living locked within my illusions, we had therefore been undoubtedly invisible to each other; the island had hardened in the space that my eyes and my will had plowed . . . ; the island had only existed through me and for me; the reality had been mine and mine alone; this unexpected Other had not only burst my world with that sole footprint, but I discovered that he exploded across the whole island in various stunning appearances; they intoxicated me with such violence that many of them began to slowly terrify me; I almost missed the idiot with the umbrella who wandered through fields and paths with a fine figure proud as a peacock; I kept coming and going, discovering and glimpsing this endless reality that stunned me like a breeze coming from the unknown abysses of my own world; I was shattered in the simplest and most literal way;

*

I experienced feelings that I had forgotten; I cried without knowing why, but what is most extraordinary, my lord, is that in front of these incredible appearances—*landscape, scents, a simple whisper, a breed of unknown goat, or a never-before-seen wild pig*—a intense feeling of surprise made me burst into laughter; I rediscovered laughter, my laugh; this phenomenon occurred one day while cautiously moving forward toward a clump of fragrant bushes; my gaze now attentive, I had noticed a tiny nest there, composed of an iridescence similar to when light touches golden wire; it was as though the bird had plucked it from some pirate's treasure somewhere on the coast, and with it he spun his fabulous dwelling; the nest was far tinier than the soft bubble that hummingbirds concocted; it was fixed in an entanglement of small branches, covered by long thorns that left no chance to the voracity of any predator; I had leaned over the small wonder, probably like a conquistador dreaming of El Dorado, when I was assaulted by a couple of birds that I could not recognize distinctly; still to this day, I am incapable of explaining what they looked like; with mind-blowing agility, they succeeded in pecking my arms, hands, forehead, and neck with such precision that I was forced into retreating; I had to jump between some tree roots, slipping under stumps on which spiders had hung goatees; and then, I began to laugh after having been panicked by such little creatures;

my first bouts of laughter came out a bit rocky, not unlike a drawn-out grumble; next, they drifted away, reminding me of the rattle of dried leaves, then the trickling of springs during the long rains; finally, they had come in a juvenile clearness that would continue to surprise me, and that seemed closer to the sound of a balafon harmonic than the prosaic movement of a larynx . . . ;

I then realized that over these twenty years my laugh had also disappeared; yet, I had maintained it lest I devolve into animality, laughing at nothing, at the empty sky, the cruel sea, laughing at the parrots, laughing when I thought about it, just to keep it functional; but it had eventually disappeared without fanfare;

while implementing my proud administration, I had closed myself to what surrounded me; in particular, I had mainly closed myself to the only human capable of hearing laughter, of reverberating it, of nourishing it this way; and this human was none other than myself; I had become an administrative machine, an exploitative strike, seeking to combat rats, cats, and termite attacks, domesticating springs and the power of the wind, tracking the slightest wear and tear of my construction and palisade, refusing disorder, hating negligence, continuously initiating projects and plans, always imagining some additional way to produce, consume, accumulate, expand, and spread on this island that served as empire and prison; I had been in true contact with nothing; and, through this harsh paradox, this absence of any contact had alienated me from myself; it is arguably at this moment that my laugh disappeared, that smiling was forgotten; now, I rediscovered them with a thrilling liveliness, much like what an idiot would harbor, but that did not bother me whatsoever; I laughed at the top of my lungs, my chest and my belly joyfully aflutter;

*

day and night, I let my laughter, tears, song, and sighs out as well as all these natural movements that had come back to each of my limbs; a common alarm bell from the depths of my being; my whole body started to live through moving gracefully, walking joyfully, and swirling my arms for no reason, my head leading the undulation of my vertebrae; my body drunk with euphoria carried me over the hills and gullies; and the wind! . . .—*oh lord, the wind!* . . .—I had become much more sensitive to the various gusts of the wind; they transported me, as if my body had been made of wings and rustling feathers; in the high-up open fields, where trees took on winding shapes to withstand the wind, walking became aerial choreography; this transformed me into a lightweight creature among the swarms of butterflies; I engaged in slow contortions with the sole desire of being in harmony with the impulses of the trade winds; I mimicked the rustling of leaves in the movement of my chest and limbs—where the headland opens out, or under the cover of grape vines—I began to blend into the spinning movements of the wind; and the wind, *my lord, the wind!* it was the crude nature of the island; it was everywhere, as much a voyager and a settler at the same time, radically foreign and familiar to the place; it came from the sea and sky, teased the unknown and was not afraid to leap into this other unknown; it lapped against trees, scraped burning rocks, skimming the ground until it had forcefully turned to dust; it was in charge of the algae, salt, dew, spring water, and a rush of promises that stood beyond the horizons; it formed an unstoppable array of scents that it emulsified in an incessant game; I was conquered; me who had until then only raised an anxious eyebrow, gauging some sort of tornado or cyclone fury, I now searched for it like an apparition, my intentions were obscure yet they unified the island in a flutter that almost seemed like some type of . . . poetry; more than ever, I dreamed of my small, mysterious book; I had always identified it as a poem; just like the book, the wind awakened in me a half-magical, half-candid vitality that bestowed the conviction of a dancer upon my feet, my backside, and my hips; thus, I danced and I was happy to do so;

*

I experienced this euphoria all day long; at night, the wind died down, giving way to gentle breezes, small creatures that spent their time nosing around; I then fed the massive fire, imagining it could be seen all over the island, and I grilled some seasoned meat; then, I conspicuously savored the candy I had brought along, hoping my Other would come out of the dark to sit with me; he never came, but at times I felt that he was there; close by; that he still did not dare; that he still did not trust me; that he needed to take his time; I thought that perhaps it emanated from myself—something unpleasant, or not engaging, probably barbaric—that kept him at a distance;

from then on, more than ever, I observed myself to make sure that my euphoria lay within joy and candidness; the staid seriousness of these last twenty years seemed dangerous; I was hungry for frivolity, I added the highest level of conformity to what constituted the substance of my soul; this attention to myself no longer confined me in any arrangement; it allowed me rather to remain free, free from time, free from maintenance, free from order and rigidity, free to do or not to do, with a liberty that brought me nearer to everything but most of all back to myself; I made an effort to radiate peacefully in a way I thought expressed all humanity; and in order to do so, I reflected deeply upon the great twenty-year abyss; my survival strategies filed past one by one illuminated by my novel perception; I reframed them within my Reasoning to rightly analyze what had transpired during this solitude; the island, my lord, had remained an airtight mass, offering but a powerful threat or the vivacity of such and such utility; my relationship to the island consisted solely of a vague despair that only this absence-presence of twenty years could express;

now, here, while contemplating at night as the embers shone gold upon an ortolan, *the island became inhabited around me;* a strange sensation; not that I no longer perceived animals, insects, or bugs, but rather *a new density* spreading in the smallest crack until invisibly emulsified; this substance consisted not only of this Other toward whom my being extended, no; it crackled with the wind; it was exploded in shapes, colors, and scents; a density that nothing could put a finger on, but that was imposed upon my entire perception; my lord, I believed that I was witnessing a crazy miracle that did not come from my elation alone, nor from this Other that drew nearer, but *from the radiating impact of the footprint;* it left more than just a simple mark on the sand; it was truly embedded within me, multiplied within my cells, and it assailed me with a wave of possible-impossibilities inconceivable until then;

I was no longer alone, the Other was here, somewhere; my feelings rose toward him as every living thing turns to face the sun; perhaps emotions and feelings must collide with identical phenomena in order to be maintained, and not just with the blue-green eye of a billy goat or with the joy that a harvest provides; no animal frenzy could know how to replace a look, a face; emotion thrives from familiarity; it is enriched in this way; the very feeling of existing emerges from this movement; that is why, over these twenty years, the feeling of my own existence had been erased within myself; or had become sporadic; it is during this drought that my laugh had disappeared, and the innocence of my eyes, and undoubtedly my desire to dance, to fool around, and to go along with the facetiousness of the wind; no matter where I looked, I only saw this frivolity, this movement, this joy, this audacity, this derailing that seized lives; *the island became inhabited around me;* first, every living thing was moved, light, frivolous, cheerful, dancing, and traveling; even the huge trees that covered a thousand leagues with only their foliage released a youthful joyfulness in the movement of their leaves . . . ;

over the first seasons of these twenty years, the feeling of my own existence had only come back in the moments of intimate collapse; without really knowing why, I started to feel sorry for myself, whining jokingly, or crying tears of distress; on this pathetic detour, I regained this sort of connection with myself; and these states undoubtedly helped me to tighten this connection because they came back cyclically, almost stably, nearly predictably; at the beginning, shocked me and I felt contrite; but I became used to letting them frolic and dissolve into the void that surrounded me: nothing and no one made sense of them; *this surrounding void had created an insidious pit deep within me,* to the extent that weeks would pass with nothing else in me but this hollow, this absence inside; I numbly watched this tearfulness come and go, arguably fighting and gaining the strength from it all the same; living alone had made me sensitive like a devastated battlefield, easily jostled by the funereal joy, the frenetic sadness, the muddy depression pushing for major projects, or by slow despair during which I sank into reading my strange little book over and over again . . . ;

but now, yes my lord, the island continued to manifest itself in a bottomless flow of apparitions of all sorts; at first they

were terrifying, then delightful, then almost wonderful, endlessly triggering a thousand images in me, sometimes dreadful,
always deeply touching; and this flow of mental images generated millions of others that arose from the trees, flowers, bees,
geckos, and any form and non-form that surrounded me; flows
fed flows; I became the shepherd of nomadic people of nomadic
images, all the while being hunted by this pack of images that
consumed my thoughts;

the sky was inhabited by birds of prey that probably should
not exist and that, I think, will never exist; the horizon reflected great harbors where tanners' hearths emitted malodor-
ous oils: I thought I had seen fortifications of coastal cities, at
times the mirage of a lighthouse beckoning me with a thousand
flashes . . . ; they shone equally in the phosphorescence of the
sea, empty for so long, which was now inhabited by great ghost
ships under massive sails;

there was no end in sight: the images were all connected, the
island linked to other islands, other cays, other banks, taking
me to moving archipelagos that I must have had visited in another life, bays, coves, cul-de-sacs, atolls of pink coral inhabited with black devils, big, noisy deltas with strange birds and
boats, wandering roots that surfaced covered in flies and layers
of mud . . . ; I felt like an entity connected to a mysterious entity; and in this connection of every thing to all things, I discovered myself as a tiny creature, yet suddenly splashed with rich
vastness;

*

floating in this tide of images, I no longer felt like a stranger before this island and its imperious vitality; nor did I feel that she
directed any hostility toward me; all this perception had done
was give me an importance that in reality I did not possess;
while searching for this Other, I transformed slowly yet constantly, I also had trouble distinguishing whether I was awake
or dreaming; throughout the seasons, in these fields, hills, landscapes, when I felt I no longer faced never-ending apparitions,

I began to find myself again, my lord, as if in front of people; I perceived very strong lives that deeply impressed me; the wind was a revenant, invisible and talkative; the waves became small cheerful girls who came to spread joy over the entire island; in front of the tall trees, wise elderly men suddenly appeared and preoccupied my mind; they held deliberative meetings that tackled the issue of my humanity; I saw wizards wearing crosses of glass, shamans with long braided hair, dignitaries bundled up in silk and sable coats; I sensed ghosts of emperors who had left their kingdom at the time of their death, and ended up in these plant fibers . . . ; actually, my lord, I sensed everything that I imagined about human beings around me in my extremely ardent invocation; the human in me not only fermented within my body but also splashed mineral shapes, trees, flowers, some animals . . . to the extent that I believed that over these twenty years, I had always unknowingly been among other human kind . . . ;

*

I saw the distance between me and various old trees, an irreducible state that forced me into imagining a humanizing shape to them, a skin-like aspect to its smooth bark, its main branch an old thigh, an eye its tree knots; I could then sympathize, and the feeling of being before someone filled me with joy;

*

I could spend moons without thinking about this Other I was searching for; his existence disappeared within me, but it was so forged from these apparitions that kept me in a state of turmoil that at no moment whatsoever would I forget him, or would I lose this imperious desire for contact with him; the most exciting phenomenon was that he gave consistency to all the parts of the island that were not under my supervision; he heightened my attention and expanded my awareness; in the haze of ubiquity, my perceptions became superimposed to cast a strange amplitude to the island; in fact, it became faster and stronger than my eyes had ever witnessed over these last twenty years; at every moment, I knew that I had been plunged into the heart of an entity that did not stop at the shores of its beaches as I had always thought; the island continued underwater, riding the waves, blending with the sky and clouds, spreading below the gullies, unfolding in the narrow passageways of caves where I had often buried my initial fears; so much space, so many depths, so many sudden perspectives, that would catch my eye and amplify it ad infinitum! . . . and all of that, without ever seeing this Other, or detecting his scent, or sensing his presence . . . ;

but on second thought, my lord, these perceptions were inherently a place of encounter; it was as if the meeting with him had already occurred; he had come toward me, I had proceeded toward him; I had imagined him in every possible way, like he would try (had he caught a glimpse of me) to imagine what I was like; this mental break afforded me a significant expanse that stretched farther and farther; wherever I wandered—the edge of a swamp, the tip of a jagged rock, the very bottom of a thicket—I extended my living space by approximately ten leagues around; my mind deemed that which was far (perceived by sound, smell, or clouded clairvoyance) as closer than the nearest thing; while that which was close from a global perspective moved away from me like another reality rising from afar; the closest and the farthest swirled around under my watchful eye; they were continuously presented below the spark of my consciousness and the ember of my imagination; thus, I was thrown into a depth and expanse that only the great hunter-warriors, or the great predators, would know, all one with the living thing that was nature; I became an animal, ears perked, nose high in the air, sniffing continuously, feeling the tree bark, touching the grain of the leaves, kneeling next to unusual poop, aware of anxiety about midges and giant rice rats, eagerly jumping at the slightest crackle, and with the ability to remain motionless amid sudden silence, seeking the source before moving on; then I started to move step by step, looking right and left, turning around suddenly, or leaping several feet to surprise, far in front of me, a brand new reality that would have vanished when approached normally;

*

on this trap of an island, I had always perceived compact hostility, demon hideouts, traps filled with wild beasts and carnivorous plants; this time, I thought I had discovered ... a colossal garden ... cultivated by an entity whose logic or intention I did not comprehend; an entity that was neither good or just or bad, but under the control of a limitless power; *and this garden belonged to no one, it was for no one;* the layout consisted of carefully planned plots and singular aptitudes organized in infinite ways—from the most extreme antagonistic violence to the closest and most innocent partnership; at times, I felt that I was being absorbed by it all, that each of my senses and actions were incorporated into it unbeknownst to me; other times, I thought I'd been expelled, and felt the urgency to act in order to find my place; but the most unpleasant feeling was to admit that ... *I was at the center of nothing;* that nothing began or ended with me; that it all decayed or renewed with or without me as I forged ahead, crossed over, and moved farther away ... ;

I did not detect the slightest solitude anywhere; these plants, rocks, and bugs did business among them, in a turbulence of exchanges impossible to identify, and even fewer to count, that was held entirely in a mass and energy, in a whole density and ephemeral flow ... ;

and things worsened, my lord; an animistic fever made me believe that appearances no longer mattered, that they were interchangeable; that in a contraction of time, space, and perception, one could pass from one appearance to another in a continuity of existences; therefore, each existence was whole and at the same time some kind of element of a whole; therefore, each death was the exact place of a rebirth that fed a whole; therefore, a whole reflected the infinite variety and diversity that existed; therefore, there were moments when I became a fern; others during which, without any despair, I had become a leaf-cutter ant; and moments when I had turned into a snake that swallowed eggs, when I was carried away by swarms of bees or loudmouthed grackles, when I started to vegetate like those large mushrooms that live off their fermentation . . . ; I was then incredibly close to the whole island; amid the turmoil of agitated sleep, *I would even become the island;* I was assailed by great oceans; I felt the crashing waves on my roaring vaults; or the peaceful foam that licked my sand-softened slopes; or their assault on the sides of my cliffs . . . but never did I experience the fear of being submerged: I perceived at the same time the meticulous patience of roots, the ground, bugs, a coalition of plants, collaboration between the sun and wind that made of me a boundless corporeal mass; in this intermittence between wakefulness and sleep, I floated in a horizontal plentitude with existence . . . ;

it came with a beautiful serenity filled with humility; for the first time in decades, I felt like I had not ended up in prison, lost and forgotten by all; what I saw was part of me like an extension of my skin, a result of heartbeats; it never stopped, even at rest (on a pile of leaves for a mattress, or in my sailor's hammock stretched between two low tree branches) when my nocturnal imagination began to fever; darkness had spread everywhere, but images hurtled with a sudden clarity in all parts of my mind; I no longer tried to free myself from this island; on the contrary: I settled, spread there, I opened myself to it with no reservations, like a cat in the morning sun; it gave me a feeling of incredible freedom, and of force in particular; a force I perceived as so healthy that I used it to spread myself even further, and to force my mind to break from its confinement; more than anything, images opened up in striking views, widening until they became exhilarating visions . . . ; I must tell you about the images, my lord . . .

the first images of my secluded life had been brought back from the frigate; I had found them in a finely built chest of such fair proportions and of such well-fitted metal hinges that water and salt were not able to penetrate; I had placed it in a corner of my cave for a few seasons, before opening it one day and discovering the material of a copyist, quills and ink (which I could use for a couple of seasons to write and make signs), but also pieces of parchment on which illumination represented landscapes: *castles, wheat fields, churches, the Virgin Mary, Christ, bridges, windmills, rivers and tributaries, herds, ladies and gentlemen, cavaliers and boats, Lancelot and King Arthur, sharecroppers, cyclopes, harpies* . . . an array of images that served as models for copyists to embellish big scholarly books; I had spent many years soaking these images up, to the extent that they had ended up becoming the world I thought I had lost; I had imagined my ancestors inside these castles, in the whirling of these windmills, and working in fields of barley or wheat; this abundance of images in so much solitude had tattooed the back of my mind; I had materialized them around me, building bridges, imitating windmills, carving my huts like old manors . . . ; now, these founding images came back in force during these sleepless nights; then, they turned cloudy and drifted away, as if they had become distorted by the strange perception that I had developed in my journey toward this Other . . .

. . . windmills began to sail . . . castles became evanescent with Oriental embellishments and plates of fine gold . . . the engraving of charming villages became cities of salt . . . nice pastureland evolved into deserts of yellow marble . . . paths made of large rocks suddenly sparkled with crystalline dew . . . ships displayed sails of great white sharkskin, deployed under reddish moons . . . parchment took refuge in bluish jars, and leather books were carried on dwarfback down the rows of a vast library located in the heart of a triangle of great lighthouses . . . in the smallest of pictograms where human beings appeared, I saw human populations, so large that they outflanked swarms of midges . . . they mixed with nocturnal insects that assailed my camp fire, or with this procession of ants that descended upon me to cut my animal pelts . . . every night with icons, images, and pictograms in mind, I journeyed without moving a muscle . . .

to experience such hallucinations, I must have spoken with old sailors, those wanderers who had seen so many places that they were ingrained on their pupils and twitching eyelids; these countries and places persisted within them, without managing to constitute a coherent whole; deserts drowned ponds; weeds overtook cities; cities swam in stormy skies, and many a ship landed on peaks or in blocks of ice; baobabs flaunted leaves of oak and cacti were laden with dates, pears, mangoes, or mandarins . . . ; under such a hullabaloo, they squinted the corners of their eyelids, and their gaze remained foggy, as though filled with antagonistic memories and crammed with emotions impossible to mistake . . . ; I had never understood this phenomenon; some people are arguably made to see no further beyond the places of their childhood; this series of discordant images that now inundated me reminded me of this unspoken drama, so much so, my lord, that I feared my dark pupils would turn white and my eyes would cross to focus on the tips of my lashes forever and ever . . . ;

in the beginning, somewhat astonished, I looked at this world of images emulsifying within me like something strange; then, I was able to let it live; then project my emotions upon it, my laughter, my desires for this flavor or that one, and parts of poems from the strange little book that I could recall; my projections had the effect of fanning the embers; this world of illusions quaked, fled, and reconstructed itself; I amplified it as I pleased, undid it in my nightmares, on the stage of my long, sleepless nights; it docilely obeyed my whims; except that, what occurred atop the wall of my sleep was unpredictable and ever improbable: blue clay cities inhabited by barefoot merchants . . . ships of rock that sailed upon huge open books brandished by men with long, white beards . . . flocks of eagles that swept along the temple pillars at the behest of a brotherhood of priests, stalks of old bamboo that resembled Buddhist monks walking in misty lands of junks and rice fields . . . ; all of this made no sense but it carried one virtue: I felt involved in their lives; despite their strangeness, I was the brother of each one; I was part of them; they navigated within me; in their company I proliferated in a pleasant space that no longer had any foundation, that no longer had any borders . . . ;

but at the end of one of these agitated nights, I realized that this Other, although nowhere to be found, materialized in each of these insane shapes; I realized they did not originate from me: it was he who provoked them; it was he whom I contemplated in these flows of illusion; this entire life, all this humanity, it was he; I reached out for him by imagining him in every possible way, in limitless shapes or boundless spaces;

*

one day, I unexpectedly found myself on an unusual beach; deprived of any sand, covered with large rocks, with only the backwash of waves and the layers of foam as a familiar point of reference; stepping closer, I nearly fainted from surprise: the beach was besieged by sea turtles; there were so many of them that not a single grain of sand was visible in this secluded cove; it was impossible to determine what they were doing—if they were laying excessive eggs or if they were engaged in a mass collective mating ritual . . . ; they may have fallen victim to a mysterious spell: they were simply here, slow, quivering, passionate, moving inch by inch, back and forth, constantly climbing over each other, in a quasi-motionless frenzy that continued to puzzle me; the beaches surveyed until then had only revealed two or three turtles; they came at night, laid eggs, and left in the glow of dawn; such numbers were never spotted, and even fewer in broad daylight . . . ;

I spent days observing these animals; their shells as wide as moons displayed small thousand-year-old rocks covered at times by clusters of oysters or dried seashells; their heads were ageless; their eyes, covered in salty brine, resembled antique glass; in my first years, I savored many a turtle; their flesh reminded me of horse that one eats on the salty shores; the best way was to cook them à l'étouffée, with a few aromatic spices; as for their eggs, they were real delicacies and a great source of strength; at that time, I wanted to slaughter one and feast upon it so as to lure the Other toward me with the aroma, but I remained still, contemplating the phenomenon; an ulterior motive told me that if this Other had also discovered this tremendous show, he could not be too far; I imagined him hiding in the bushes, fascinated as I was by this mass of life that toiled over some sacred mystery; birds came from the horizons to frolic among the shells, hopping on heads, picking at scales; an abundance of red crabs imitated them, hoisting large yellowish claws presented to the sky like countless violins; the contribution from the bugs was an excitement that spread throughout; all of this created an organism that replaced the beach itself, inhaling the swash of the swell and the assault of the foam; without really comprehending, I removed the pelts that covered my shoulder, keeping but a piece of the soft leather that I usually tied around my waist and my loins; then, I slipped down into, like the birds and crabs, the entanglement of shells . . . ;

bugs dispersed as I approached, but the turtles ignored me completely; I worked up the courage and started to climb them, contorting myself like a mollusk, embracing their humps, roundness, and hollows, and moving forth between them, on top of them, along with them, eager to have such a closeness with these impenetrable creatures; I wanted to experiment stopping between them, and staying still, and seeing how this organism with a thousand heads, beaks, and sad eyes started to slowly crawl over me, just as each turtle crawled over each other . . . ; I saw powerful legs pass by, and scaly, yellowish bellies; heads slid under my neck, and pupils stared blankly at me; over time, I tried to look at them the same way they looked at me; my back must have surely had to bow and be covered in scales . . . ; I glued my whole body onto each turtle, then experienced a curious sensation, truly carnal, that spread over my skin like a shiver, and that filled my belly once again with a lost twinge . . . ; my penis must have stood up, erupting in jerks, and then relaxed, and I began to lick the turtles, which filled me with a taste of algae, rotten salt, and dead shellfish . . . ; I soon became covered with their tears and sticky drool, to the point

of suffocation, which forced me to rapidly pull myself out to
rejoice in the waves . . . ;

arbitrarily happy, I contemplated the phenomenon; it became
even more mysterious given what I had experienced from the
inside; I imagined this Other had witnessed the display; that
he must have certainly taken me for a fool; this possibility did
not bring me any shame; I was actually rather happy with it; it
brought him closer to me, just as I had become vaguely closer
to him while clinging to these turtles . . . ; to hold them, touch
them, had been like holding him, touching him . . . ;

I could have spent the rest of my life there as the spectacle was
so captivating, but I understood that the turtles and I did not
live in the same time; their lives here resulted from an endless
slowness, of an eternal loop impossible to comprehend and that
could have swallowed me whole had I wanted to grasp any
meaning or some sort of outcome from it . . . ; I left for the
peaks that stood above the seagrapes; as I turned my back on
it, I had the impulse to name that beach—I considered: "Beach
of the Eternal Turtle"—but I kept quiet, erased the name from
my mind, thus forcing myself to keep this encounter in its wild,
pure state . . . ;

*

it must have been the day of blows to the heart; I had just
cleared the seagrapes, reaching a field of spicy herbs, scented
like hot peppers and spangled with red pompoms, when I came
to be assailed by a swarm of grackles; as black and shiny as the
devil, these birds tempted to peck my eyes out; I resisted the
impulse to issue warning shots; I was reaching the end of my
powder reserves, and lead shots were scarce—so scarce that I
had replaced them with shards of seashell; the winged devils
followed me for several leagues, as if they were trying to expel
me from a forbidden kingdom; this phenomenon intrigued me
so much that I quickly turned back, taking care to perform a
large, protective circle; I approached this field diagonally, so as

to conveniently examine it with my telescope; its thorny shrubs were filled with nests; they were tangled with dry branches and big thorns; fibers similar to spiderwebs forged them to leaves so tightly that the wind could no longer make anything quiver; and these nests were populated with small, famished beings of all species, such that a cloud of grackles and dozens of birds incessantly came and went to feast upon them with indifference; an immense incubator lay before me like an impregnable fortress; the bird-keepers hunted rats, cats, snakes . . . but also sand-hares, apple-foxes, short-legged wolves—all these unknown predators to whom I had given a name due to a vague resemblance and in accordance with my discretionary power; the place remained under extreme vigilance; nothing could enter; the slightest movement at its borders triggered a concert of boos and wing flapping that struck the area . . . ; here again, I was dazed in contemplation; for a long while, with no impatience whatsoever . . . ; perhaps hoping deep in my soul that this automatic alarm would manage to reveal this Other to me sooner or later, the invisible one; I prayed to the heavens that he be led right to this place . . . ;

it was not the first time that I had been attacked by birds; during my first wheat harvest, multitudes of birds and seven species of rats had come running to my field; tempted by the fully matured ears of wheat, they had begun a sort of siege in a strange concert; all had set up camp there, day, night, rain, wind, fighting to steal grain at every given opportunity; I was forced to spray them with bullets time and again, even to use a trebuchet; out of desperation, and for the sake of preserving my ammunition, I had put up a horde of jingling scarecrows that were able to contain the most impressionable ones; they settled all around me, with niches, nests, and luggage; it had been guerilla warfare to collect a few calabashes of wheat—I used then a sickle forged from a pirate saber—before they gobbled everything; the hostility of this island was found in the fury of these birds and rats; they attacked together, one taking advantage of the audacity of the others; later, I carefully reinforced my fields so as to avoid such accumulation, to the extent that, despite the countless losses caused by these creatures, I had always been able to store enough of it as the seasons went by to prepare nice warm bread, or cooked buckwheat pancakes that started to crisp in a clay oven . . . ; there, on the lookout, waiting for my Other to be caught in the trap, each alert made me jump, eager to finally discover him in a swarm of enraged creatures . . . ; over the weeks I was camped there, thousands of creatures were attacked by the grackles . . . but not him . . . never him;

*

continuing my investigation, I had embarked on a steep slope, one that lead to the great peaks; these places are very pleasant, deprived of mosquitoes and of the heat that causes fevers; I found various types of raspberries there, and other delicious berries that I gulped endlessly; dark purple prunes grew in abundance, smaller than the prunes I had known; they turned the tongue blue, chilling the teeth and leaving a flavor of turpentine on the taste buds; after identifying their blooming season, I had cleaned out these places regularly; this time again, I delighted in the idea of eating raspberries and attempted to convince myself that this Other must have discovered them too, and that he lingered here carelessly; I therefore prepared to surprise him during his feast, to share them with him, when I stumbled upon something incredible: *a small rice field, fluttering under the caress of the trade winds* . . . ; it had emerged in the waters that streamed from the peak and that rocks retained in basins filled with humus; it took some time for me to understand this miracle, until I remembered that one day, as I was chased by wild pigs, I had hurtled down this slope, falling flat on my back, and smashed a few of the calabashes that hung from my waist; these little travel containers constituted my reserves of seeds and seedlings that I had brought back from the frigate; while falling, I had scattered half a peck of rice seeds, certainly intended for a more favorable area on the other side of the island; no matter how much I had dragged myself flat on my stomach, scrutinizing moss, checking cracks, searching for seed after seed, I only managed to recover a pathetic pinch that I was never able to fructify; this accident had escaped my mind; so, on this very day, I discovered this bed of rice plants, perfectly green, thriving, filled with water, healthy and crispy; it had adapted to a higher elevation, to this humus mixed with volcanic ash, and to the incessant water flows; it was here, like a mirage;

I took this discovery as if the whole island were winking at me; I wondered how many surprises it had then left in my wake, without my being aware; with the vestiges of that world from the ship that I personally deemed Noah's Ark, I had surely fertilized it over and over by accident and in my clumsiness; I cried over this incongruous rice field; there again, as if my body now regulated my perception, I lay naked among the small sprouts, softly touching them, counting them, scrutinizing them one by one; I delighted in imagining them fully grown, ripened, carried in my wicker basket, threshed from the stalk, and I salivated over the idea that I would soon taste rice cakes once more . . . ; while I brushed against the small sprouts, a strange sensation traveled across my skin, shiver by shiver; it awoke my body in a way that I had forgotten; I would have been so proud for this Other, the invisible one, to appear suddenly, for him to see me, celebrating the accidental fertilization, this perfect unintentional work . . . ;

to think about him, in this miracle rice field, amplified each angle of my gaze, each flash of my consciousness; I was fully examining this new wonder; my body, my eyes, my thoughts, and my mind experienced an unordinary harmony, *a silent perspicacity;* I no longer babbled in my mind; I was present in the present, with such acuteness that I imagined these lost seeds, lonely, struggling in the moss and humus, absorbing these strange waters, opening their alchemies to odd hostilities, experimenting with an avant-garde germination, and growing so cautiously in order to strengthen at the slightest opportunity; I also saw the movement of the sap catching the sun, how the fibers and matrices spread, and the seed itself, which for me represented nice, warm rice cakes and delicious croquettes, mixed with sugarcane juice and coconut cream; *I was alive among these living sprouts;* this state had me so bothered that images of women's bodies filled my head, mixed with turtle shells, swarms of grackles, velvety moss upon extraordinary tree trunks; past romances, lips, breasts, and eyes, and vulvas, hints of intimate body parts . . . ; when I got up, I was thirsty, hungry, hypersensitive as ever, and in total need of everything; I eagerly set off again searching for this invisible Other; I went as I was, drunk, ethereal, stumbling, clumsy yet agile, as if in love but with no one to love, just with this awakening that love procures for us; I was kicked out of myself, my lord, full of imaginary desire and desire-imagining . . . ;

*

I spared my efforts much less than I felt them at all; after walking past the same places over and over, and although I kept experiencing surprises at each passage, I recognized I had just gone around the island four or five times; it was not so big that each step opened my perception to enormities; I decided to initiate a new search, focusing this time on sites likely to shelter my invisible Other pleasantly; I therefore explored well-known caves, unearthing others, and at the same time visited those in which I had stocked war supplies; all were welcoming, always cool, offering church-like atmospheres; in one of them, I discovered an extraordinary colony of flying rats; they had invaded the place for thousands of years; the ground was covered with their fabulous guano, and their urine emitted a smell that asphyxiated me right away; I fell backward with surprise and I had to crawl for twenty-five cubits before running for my life . . . ;

in another cave, I found a new underground spring that at the very beginning had made me feel delighted; I had considered turning it into a steam room, with the idea of coming here for respite to bathe, inhale perfumes, meditate upon the strange little book . . . ; I had stored a few bamboo sticks to dry on a platform of pebbles there, in order to subsequently build a comfortable pallet, and trays on which I could arrange a few wax candles; but emergencies had pulled me away from this project and I had not come back for many long years; the bamboo was still there, dried like I had hoped; the spring gurgled at the very bottom of the cave, in the rift of a black rock where traces of yellow sulfur could be spotted; around it, shiny clay filled the cracks, and gave life to whitish moss able to survive without much light; the cave entrance was a narrow hole; the rays of the sun painstakingly slipped inside to become but an imaginary clarity; the ceiling showed constant collapses, but it seemed solid in this assembly of rocks welded together by roots; the latter sending out lateral roots that striated the walls with translucent inlets toward the ground; I explored its corners and narrow passageways: my Other was not there; despite it all, I stood still for a while in this place; the dark calmed me, and abated this stream of images that flooded my mind; I had to go to sleep . . . to be awakened by the feeling of something brushing past me; I immediately thought it was the Other . . . with dazzling speed, I saw him sneak silently through the cave . . . discovering me . . . kneeling beside me . . . smiling . . . and touching my arm to wake me . . . ; I jumped to my feet in a mix of terror and desire, only to discover . . . that tortoises . . . venerable lives, were trundling emotionless toward the spring . . . ;

tortoises were abundant on the island; I had adopted a few of them; I liked their slow motion, their way of living without any imperious desires or pressing urges; they did it all at their own pace; if things accelerated around them, they retracted their heads, closed the hatches, and waited for the storm to pass; I jostled several of them, forced some to hurtle down slopes, stoned others with shells; how long they remained motionless depended on the trauma, playing dead until they were forgotten; then one realized they had gone; perhaps I had experienced a tortoise-crisis, moving slow, defying time, making sure to dismantle it, confining myself in an inner immobility waiting for the long-desired help that I desperately needed to fill the horizon and rescue me; as I could not leave this island, nor could I resign myself to meeting my fate here, only time was accessible, only time could I possibly slow down or stop . . . ; in my magic against time, I had turned myself into a tortoise . . . ; and therefore, it was a sign for me to find them here, at the very moment where I had never been so far from them; I was ebullient with energy, speed, and force, impatient to unearth this Other and finally return to the Human species; the tortoises, on the other hand, trotting toward the spring, undoubtedly with just as much appetite, continued without any excitement, impassively resolute and serene; the island coming to my rescue through these old tortoises, progressing step by step toward the song of the spring, my lord: *it reminded me of the cost of patience and beauty of slowness . . .* ;

*

it is in the last cave that I thought I would find him; the cave was located at the edge of the shore, in a former riverbed where leafless shrubs that had been plucked by the wind grew and searched for sustenance in the sandy, rocky ground; the cave opened to the side of a hill, like a gaping wound whose prickly weeds would have healed lips; in olden times, I had discovered it effortlessly because it was visible from the beach; I had stocked it with two muskets, some powder, two or three lead shots, and dried fruits that I could not find elsewhere, probably claimed by the local creatures; I always reached these places with the excitement of discovering one of my tracks, as if, as proof of my original activities, these tracks allowed me to introduce an old-me to the one I had become; the cave was bright, peppered with dark spots that indicated deeper guts; as soon as I entered, I felt something; at the very back; motionless; I called: *Who is there?! Is it you, my friend? . . . Peace, peace, friend, friend . . .* ; as he remained silent, I presumed his fear and set about appeasing him; I told him my name; I told him how long I had been living on this island; in case he did not understand my language, I took several gentle, friendly, benevolent bows and I kept the palms of my hands open; I wanted to tell him about discovering his footprint, and the many seasons I spent looking for him, but I fell silent very quickly, and concentrated on approaching in the most normal way possible, hoping then to defuse any tension; he moved in the darkness, drifting to the left; when I leaned left, he shifted strongly to the right; I believed he was in pain, probably injured, and suddenly I understood why it had been so difficult to find him; chased by his cannibal brothers, he had washed ashore on this island on the back of a skiff; he had then rushed into this shelter to hide and heal his wounds; they must have been deep for him to stay here for so long and to be so weak; my arsenal of medicines, accumulated over several years, ran through my mind; I had leaf pastes for compound fractures; honey balms for burns; beet syrup for chest pains; decoctions of rum, tobacco, and lemon, powerful for healing and scarring; I had tonics for blood, something to heal scabies and itches; and a set of ointments that I had recovered from the frigate that must have belonged to the surgeon onboard; with their faded labels, these flasks had remained real mysteries in regards to their virtues and uses; at times I had spread some of it on cuts at random, or tasted it when a fever occurred, but with so much frugality that it never made a difference; nevertheless, I felt like I could get what- or whomever back on their feet; I started to explain these remedies to him when I heard a moan; there was nothing human about it, my lord; I felt something painful in my mind; I jumped on the thing so as to ward off bad luck—but this was indeed misfortune: it was not him, but an old manatee; the animal must have surely have dragged himself here to die; he was just skin and bones, and limp with old age, and perhaps at the beginning of the species' extinction; its skin was eaten by an unknown leprosy, his gaze only mournful supplications; it all stopped instantly when I broke its neck; and then I fled from that cave . . . ;

*

after each disappointment, the certainty that he was here, right in front of me, next to me, not far, got me back on my feet; I stopped at coves that were immediately designated havens of peace; there were recessions of cliffs filled with sand that the sea had fertilized with a variety of plants; these hard-to-access, secluded coves were teeming with fish; white mullets and huge, flat crabs lay dormant there beneath the foam; schools of multicolored carp proliferated at the very edge of the shore; in these kinds of places, I had gone rifle fishing until I started to ration my bullets; I had subsequently crafted a set of hooks from frigate nails; I always had some in my travel bag; I armed them at the end of a very thin and resistant woven fishing line, and I fished by hooking shellfish that had stuck to the cays; that day, I had barely thrown my bait when I felt an enormous jolt; I figured out what it was: one of those slimy snake-fish with jaws of steel that camped outside the rocks to ambush octopuses; how dreadful that such a creature became ensnared in my bait; they were never easy to reel in; their body is a muscle that rolls up into the cays, and they brace so firmly that it is impossible to pull them out, unless the hook causes them to drown; I fought with it for I do not know how long; darkness was already falling when it suddenly stopped resisting, possibly sustaining a heart attack; I then pulled out a slimy, spotted, greenish, scaly dragonfish, much bigger than my arm, and close to seven feet long; a real monster that must have lived here for thousands of years; I quickly cleaned it as the day faded into night; on a fire of almond tree stalks, I grilled large sections of it; its meat was white, thin, and of exquisite flavor, between rabbit and poultry; I added a few dry spices from my calabashes, and savored it thinking about this Other on some lookout; I shouted at him in all directions that he was wrong and it was a feast; and I smiled, even laughed as I shared the leftovers with the crabs, and I settled onto a bed of leaves, after drinking a sip of rum that I resorted to in order to face the assault on my mental images and senses;

*

at daybreak, I continued my journey, treading more slowly; something had changed; I no longer searched for my Other with the same intensity; the desire to find him was still as strong, the desire ever-present in my mind, but I did it . . . with restraint; as if I feared the search were exhausted, forcing myself to admit that he was nowhere to be found . . . and that he would remain as such forever and ever;

in the throes of agony, I imagined he had just disembarked, and embarked once again a few moments later, leaving only the footprint pointing toward the interior of the island; but I quelled this despondency by convincing myself that he was here, he was a castaway, that a tree stump had brought him here like the many tree stumps that suddenly appeared from the ocean loaded with creatures that had come from afar; once, I had seen a monkey with white and ochre fur disembark from fragments carried by the current; he had stamped the sand in a sort of dance before running off to the nearest trees; I had never seen his kind among the monkeys of the island, but a few seasons later, I could recognize him in tens of little monkeys that blended their fur with white and ochre: they reflected the genitor that the ocean had brought . . . ; I repeated this self-evident fact: *the island was welcoming, and only welcoming, made up of luck, encounters, and hospitality;* I proceeded toward this Other with these stanzas in my head, forcing me to believe, yet unable to find him anywhere, nurturing the enthusiasm I wanted to foster . . . ;

*

one day, I made the decision to return to the footprint, not to convince myself once more of its presence, but to celebrate what it had sparked in my mind and life; I found it right where I had left it, with its share of subtle transformations that continuously affected the beach; that day, I saw it when the position of the sun showed its lateral forms, and outlined it more clearly; I lay down once again next to it to interrogate the petrifaction that immortalized it; the sand was inhabited by a blackish clay that tended to harden and crack; the clay here kept the sand from scattering; while it appeared to be flexible, the clay maintained a shape so tightly that no rain, foam, or gust of wind could erode it; this persistence was truly a wonder; taking a closer look, I saw that jellyfish slime was spread in the clay; its surface was greyish, haunted with whitish or bluish concretions; I smiled when I looked at it; probably laughed too; really happy it was here, that it radiated with such intensity that it continued to expand within me; it was a rift in the reality that until then I had decreed on this island; I had come across such rifts at the foot of old volcanoes from which the ends of the earth glowed bright red; the footprint gave me the same feeling: it survived on iron-clad intensity; it brooded over forces; and better yet: it became the crater of an eruption that only I received, in the stomach, in the heart, in the mind; the footprint shook me profoundly, alerted the invisible, disrupted possibilities and impossibilities; how I laughed at the image that kept spinning in my mind: *the island was giving birth here, and gave birth to me as well . . .*

I feared a storm would destroy the beach and take the footprint away forever; its disappearance would return me to a solitude that I was now incapable of bearing; I ran like a madman into the woods, collecting fibrous, flexible fiddlewood branches that took on the consistency of iron in the hot sun; I had often used them to support my network of pipes, raise wind turbines, uphold fragile caves; with the stems, I built a hut on top of the footprint that I covered with sugarcane leaves; the finished scaffolding looked like a real little hut; weathered by the sun, the sugarcane straw started to grow pale, and soon took on this creamy layer that nothing could penetrate, not water, nor wind, nor heat; the hut cast a shady square of protection onto the footprint, shielding it from the sun's heat, the hammering rain, and the relentless winds from the south;

I started to think as I watched the waves crash a few inches from the footprint; the tide was not strong in this area and could never reach the footprint, but a swell coming from the depths of the ocean would sweep it away in one blow; so close to the shore, it is impossible to fight the ocean's anger; I nevertheless tackled the task of building a dike by collecting pink rocks that gathered at the bottom of a cliff one by one; I piled them up straight in a channel of more than twenty cubits, until they formed a low wall a *toise* high; I cut a series of long stakes that I hammered flush with the low wall just behind it, as if it were leaning against it, and making the most of this support, I do not know how many moons and suns I spent moving blocks of rock; they soon formed, between the footprint and the sea, an impressive rampart that reached my shoulder; I began transporting sand in large calabashes (normally dedicated to salting fish and meat); to reinforce the rampart with stakes, I amassed a ridge of sand, sprayed with seawater, that I covered with flat rocks and dried turtle shell; the fortification was a solid source of comfort; then, in the shade of the scaffolding, nestled into a small throne, I was able to sip on my flask of rum or macerate various fruit pulps; the fruits sustained the burn of the alcohol in a mixture of flavor that created an explosion in every direction; I remained this way for countless seasons, the philosopher and suckler, all while blissfully contemplating the footprint . . . ;

*

this proximity to the footprint triggered my imagination even more; I saw the indent of the heel, the bulge of the arch of the foot, the fanning of toe prints, and this brought back memories of shores, countries, people, songs, dancing, books, love, food cravings, sighs, smiles, and words exchanged in bed . . . a whole mess that befuddled my mind and removed me both from the flow of time as well as from the density of the island that surrounded me; at times, I came back to reality, surprised to find that I had dozed with my eyes open; other times, I regained consciousness in a state of trembling; I then realized I had not eaten anything for far too long, and I began to drowsily look for fruits and some calabashes of water in my immediate vicinity; I was not extremely inclined to get back to my cave; I had become a sedentary person next to the footprint, and when, being able to tear myself away, I came back to my main base to collect some supplies and clothes, I was always surprised to find that weeds had proliferated, and rats burgeoned shamelessly . . . ; a bunch of animals swarmed fearlessly in my belongings, but it did not affect me much; *I let the island take its course;* I left the island to its excesses; I did nothing more than reinforce the protection of my vital resources, checking on how diverse mechanisms functioned; my farm animals had rediscovered their natural instinct of feeding themselves on their own, but they remained in herds next to the pens and pastures, as if they were bound to the order I had established over the years; I just made sure that they saw me and I left right after; coming back to the footprint, I first and foremost checked my low, protective wall, fortifying it day after day, piece by piece, whether it needed it or not . . . ;

soon, I began to search specifically for unusually colored rocks; indigo, mauve, bright red, and jade green; I also gathered seashells with sumptuous mother-of-pearl, which I shattered to collect the most beautiful pieces, and arrange them artistically atop the low wall, giving it multicolored reflections; the wall radiated in the sun and full moons made it sparkle like the dome of a Byzantine palace; the rest of the time, I brought back calabashes with the darkest, richest soil, which I pushed into the cracks of the rocks, and I planted my perennials with all their roots; many of them dried out in the sun, and the others began to vegetate under the violence of this exile; but, when the rains returned, they started to bloom, and the low wall was brought to life; a jumble of colors and scents that attracted bees, dragonflies, butterflies . . . ; these insects paid an extremely cheerful tribute to the footprint by way of their buzzing . . . ; in the soil I had brought, there must have been many types of germs; unexpected undergrowth swamped the pink rocks and mother-of-pearl shells, transforming the low wall into a mineral-plant-covered hedge; I made sure to pull the weeds capable of growing into trees, their overly powerful roots would have compromised the structure; soon, the stacks of rocks disappeared, revealing only here and there touches of pink and mother-of-pearl shells that emerged like mineral flowers from the shimmer of the leaves; ground-cover plants grew from the low wall to cover the hill of sand just behind the stakes, and germinated very quickly where they could; the rampart largely represented an achievement I could not stop marveling over; leaning back against the sand dune, beneath the small hut, I had finalized my makeshift throne with large cushions of fragrant herbs, comfortable to my

liking; I sat there for hours doing nothing, daydreaming, hum-
ming, scratching my belly button, and of course contemplating
this striking footprint; the flowers on the wall attracted hummingbirds; swarms of banaquits came to rummage with their
beaks; lizards, like so many other creatures, had left the trees
and were getting by, as if they were fascinated by this hanging jungle; migrating crabs sometimes climbed the wall and
seabirds used it for an observation post . . . ; the footprint was
surrounded with exciting life that illustrated exactly what was
deep inside me . . . ;

I soon had to fight flowering vines; they invaded the mound,
and rolled out like a carpet across the burning sand; they died,
decomposed, and new vines sprouted from the peat that was
created; they entangled skillfully, to the extent that their vol-
untary destruction and intricacy produced compost for the sole
purpose of their expansion; I was fascinated by this plant life: it
fed on itself and kept growing, and fostered its longevity alone
in perpetuity; I had grabbed my sickle and, letting the vine grow
anywhere else, I channeled it to respect the footprint; I made a
clear three-cubit circle around the footprint and the hut, and
not a day went by without weeding, cutting, pulling, scraping,
or cleaning . . . ; I could not stop coming and going, or stamping
around the footprint . . . ;

that is when the worst happened, my lord; one rainy day, the
sand being wet, I let the rain showers drain off, and while back
at work I realized I saw something that shook me to the core:
there was another footprint here; it had just been molded; I
threw myself upon it, looking at it closely, looked around me,
and saw nothing other than the sand furrowed by my own
stomping; the rain, on the other hand, helped the new footprint
to be better outlined; no matter how closely I looked at it, it
resembled the other one; I remained petrified for long periods,
dismissing any thoughts, forbidding my imagination its wild
theories; verily, I attempted to petrify everything in my heart
but this organ seemed to have its own perceptive ways; it therefore began to palpitate irregularly; when I was able to extricate

myself from this anxious astonishment, great fatigue befell me, made of doubt, explosive clarity, refusal, and fear; and it is with immeasurable slowness that I did what I had never thought of doing throughout this whole adventure; I stood, and approaching the footprint that I had just discovered, I placed my foot into it: a perfect fit; I then turned around and pushed the hut over in one fell swoop of my arm, and I towered above the mysterious footprint; trembling, I stuck my foot out, my lord, put it down, while my heart melted, tears overflowed from my heart and gushed from my eyes and ears; my foot fit the footprint so well that I could no longer deny that this mysterious footprint was my very own;

I screamed in despair like a stuck pig; I fell to my knees on the footprint and began to destroy it along with its final lie; I rolled on it crying like a baby; in my tearful rage, I destroyed the mound of sand, the rampart of stakes; tackling the wall, I fluttered the rocks around, one by one, as far as I could in the foamy bubbles; I begged the ocean to come and submerge this beach and forever erase everything that had happened here; in this agitation, I vainly tried to suppress an old, persistent, and familiar terror; I was alone, a thousand times alone, I had always been, and I would forever be on this forgotten island . . . ;

*

yet, I stayed on this beach, as if I were waiting for a miracle from the abyss of despair; countless seasons may or may not have gone by, either way; I was physically and emotionally exhausted much like in the collapses of my first years; I had curled up at the foot of a seagrape tree; a shady area where the sand was unbelievably white; there, motionless, just chewing on grapes that I had picked merely by raising my hand; hundreds of yellowish, bright red, little crabs went back and forth across my belly and legs; they had become used to my paralysis; I gave them the impression that I was no longer alive, which was not wrong; a leaden solitude crushed me entirely; it was asphyxiating; my body had become immense; I was compressed deep down into it, as if attempting to break from the rigid anguish my body conveyed to me; and if I kept this open perception that made me empathetic toward the environment, I fought like the devil against the feeling of my body closing upon me like the mouth of a prison; sometimes, I summoned this collection of images that, since the footprint, had awoken my mind; their origin had dried up; the ones that came back in a macabre dance were tarnished with déjà vu; these images floated in my mind with the tune of a ripped music score incapable of sustaining any sort of melody; shooing them from my mind, I looked around me, with one eyelid closed and deprived of light; the beach that extended in motionless sparkles; tortuous trunks of seagrape trees, sharply cutting through the sun and shade; their rounded leaves, made for rolling cones to hold grapes; olive trees that flaunted these poisonous fruits to the old manchineel trees over and over . . . ; everything was vitrified by the sun; each detail an archive of sadness and futurelessness; disillusioned, my lord;

I thought back upon the wonderful places I had roamed while I searched for this illusory Other; that which had amazed me had lost its charm; very quickly, it became harder and harder to imagine the island as a whole, to reconstruct in my mind this round shape that I had surmised, these mountainous paths, its backwaters, its thickets of thousand-year-old trees that erased the sky . . . all of that disappeared into an improbable mist . . . all of that was forgotten little by little . . . ; what I perceived of this island now remained in my periphery; the island was nothing more than this beach where I now found myself; seagrapes, crabs, sand, foam, metallic horizon, empty sky . . . ; my heart grew heavy once more as certain places resonated like hollow, busted jars; despite myself, the old sordid hope began to torment my soul; my eyes lingered over the skyline in hopes of seeing the glint of a sail emerge, or to glimpse an unusual break in the relentless blue—these images that provoke the sudden appearance of an invisible ship; this plea to the horizon had consumed me for decades, with the capacity to cause incredible harm, and now, it reared its ugly head in resentment; I pushed it away with all my might, but this drive was but a flea in dire straits in a dazed body; I no longer had much energy at the heart of this disaster;

the other hope that lay within me was that I had fallen victim to a bout of delusion; it was possible that the footprint did not fit my foot so well . . . ; I would sometimes contemplate the idea—with great force—that this Other who had landed here was my age, my size, had the same size feet, and that I gave in too quickly to despair . . . ; life was filled with ambivalence; reality was made up of differences, but in this web of differences persisted curious similarities, coincidences, and fabulous contingencies . . . ; to see it that way comforted me a bit; I once again began to entertain the idea that this impossible Other was still here, somewhere; but, in moments of clarity, I gave up on this improbability: there was no small boat; no man-bearing skiff had washed ashore anywhere; no other footprint had appeared anywhere . . . ; I dwelled on pathetic thoughts, forged convictions only to discredit them right away; I ended up reminding myself of when I had stripped the frigate; the wreckage had washed ashore on the cays directly opposite this beach; while bringing back the spoils on a creaky, makeshift raft, I had frequently disembarked and walked, right where the footprint was located; it was certainly my own; petrified here, surely during my last trip, just before the frigate moved, and remained here for decades, just to throw me into one final despair . . . ;

*

the generous extensions of my mind waned; reducing the amount of dreams, illusions, disdain, fortunate mistakes, and beliefs; it dried up, now incapable of creating or perceiving any apparitions; I saw my mind subsisting on the surface of an opaque backwater, like the eyes of a deceased toad that would soon reach the seafloor, and end up as silt in the thin mud . . . ;

*

the day I found the strength to stand up, my lord, I headed once more toward the footprint; the entire area had been wrecked, stomped on; all that remained were ruins of the small hut and debris of pink rocks interspersed in the foam; the sand had mixed with the waves; the mound had disappeared; no more footprint; nothing left; only crabs, algae, the heat haze, and dust blowing in the wind; I was truly alone; for no reason, I screamed my name in anger, *Crusoe! Robinson Crusoe!* ... and I pounded my chest while swearing at the heavens; Here I was ... alone ... it was just me! ... ; I projected this image of *myself* all across the horizon in a web of delusional curses ... ;

I suddenly held my tongue, and repeated: "myself!" ... ; I repeated it over and over again in various tones, with multiple emphases that I stressed on whichever syllable; and as if I were trying to convince myself of my own existence, I patted my arms, chest, and head after brushing aside tufts of hair; here I was; I was myself, myself, myself! ... ; and I cried over the idea of "self"; the misleading appearance of the Other had thrown me off; the disappearance of the cursed footprint suddenly sent me right back to it; I ruminated over this like the entrance of a prison; I did not want to take refuge in it, and at the same time this deadly solitude forced me to search for some company, another "self" for reassurance; I cried over the idea, which contained all the misery in the world; the loneliness on this island could not bear a "self," it ended up annihilating it in its mirage and empty mechanisms; I learned this the hard way as I had become a radiating idiot ... ; yet, with the disappearance of the footprint, this "self" was my unique perspective, the only infinitesimal space that I could navigate with the tiniest bit of movement, the onset of an impulse; I smiled at the idea of an imperceptible movement—it was all worth more than the immobility of purposeless solitude, and of the death that comes with it ... ;

on my knees, I began to carefully pat myself all over; not feverishly as I had done upon discovering the footprint, but ever so slowly, desiring to feel; I caressed the skin of my arms, wrinkled, old, burned by the salt and sun; I felt its texture, pinched myself, ran my fingers across the dry skin; I then patted my entire body, squatting in the sand; I reached for my neck, felt the flow in my veins, and got closer to . . . my face; strange that I had not thought of it for a long time . . . *my face* . . . I could not even remember the last time I had attended to it over these dark years . . . with some hesitation, I first patted my head, where I found old little bumps and a few scars; then I examined my neck before slowly coming back toward my forehead; struck by an odd apprehension, I suddenly moved toward my thighs, knees, and remained there for a good bit, without thinking, just paying attention t what my hands perceived; and once again, slowly, I returned to . . . the face that I supposed was mine; I began to feel a chin, lips, a nose, cheeks, an arch supporting my thick brows . . . ; as I discovered these shapes, my heart rate increased; suddenly, I stopped abruptly and shook my hands as if they had touched something indecent . . . ;

the idea of the mirror came back to me; I wanted drive it out as I was very afraid of that mirror I had kept; I had collected it in a lady's cabin in the forecastle; a beautiful object that had unfortunately shattered in the shipwreck; I had removed the frame and salvaged a shard large enough to use; I had experienced the first trauma when the reflection in the shard of mirror did not remind me of anyone; a stranger had appeared to contemplate me just as I contemplated myself; helpless, I had put it back in one of my storage chests; then, I had forgotten it; I had taken it back out many months later, attempting to reflect the sunlight to attract ships that I thought I saw drifting a few cables away; then, I had put it back once more; it glittered in the light when attached to my waist, provoking more and more unbearable hallucinations; over the past few years, while exploring my reserves, I had often come across this shard of mirror without paying it too much mind or peering into it to look at myself; seeing my face was of no interest; first, it forced me to confront the great abyss of my forgotten past; then, after fully becoming Robinson Crusoe, I had no longer needed to see that face, or even imagine it; finally, in my struggles against animality, I was convinced that my face had died, and that my eyes no longer reflected life; when I happened to glimpse myself in the mirror, it remained such a shock for me that I ended up inadvertently avoiding it; I had convinced myself that facial movements only functioned among human beings; *that a face was only what it had retained from encountering others;* my parrots, or that dog rescued from the frigate—which had accompanied me for a few years—had not needed to see my face to sense my feelings; they merely considered my eyes, gestures, scent, all these things still reflected the remnants of my soul; for a long time, I had been only an omniscient administrator of this island, a great founder of civilization without equal; I had eventually dissolved within this mental image; and if I had stood up so straight, dressed in animal pelt, parasoled, armed, eager to perform inviolable rituals, it was probably because I attempted to establish a structure to this increasing process of denaturing that made me into a part of the island; from then on, if I had happened to call upon this shard of mirror, it was for an extremely rare, special event during which I celebrated the island's Constitution by reading it in its entirety; I then took the mirror out from somewhere in storage, put it on the table beneath the kapok tree, positioned it to reflect nothing in particular, for some eye of eternity, the auspicious ceremony that I always regretted no one could witness . . . ;

and therefore, thinking about the mirror on that day, I ran toward my main cave and started to rummage through my stores, baskets, countless boxes, chests and cases, lifting shambles of odd objects that I had not made use of, or that I had vaguely used before putting them back; despite how I may have torn through everything in a quivering fever, visiting most of my annexes, I never managed to find that illustrious shard; I exited like a madman to head to the nearest pond; while in solitude, I had also avoided ponds smooth enough to spot my silhouette in the water; this time, I looked hard in an attempt to examine this face of mine; the water was cloudy and grey during this season, and it did not reflect clearly enough to show what I had hoped to see; I came back to the cave where I grabbed a tin saucepan, I polished it as best as I could in an attempt to see myself, but the tin, dotted by salt, only reflected a vague blob; all I had left were my hands, which I used to explore this part of myself; what I felt beneath my fingertips—lips, eyebrows, nose, forehead, cheeks, chin, grimaces . . .—only caused my heart to panic; my mind recognized none of these forms that my fingers conveyed to me; I was not able to identify my face as a whole, or draw the slightest familiarity from it; my face felt completely foreign to me; I was aware that my memory lapses had erased everything about my own "person," but such radical alterity emerging from the most fundamental part of me was difficult to accept; I lived in a stranger's body;

I spent several days getting to know my face, feeling it, imagining it over and over; at times I found myself noble and handsome, a well-defined jaw and a high forehead, with the allure of a fleet admiral or a pirate prince; other times, I sensed something swollen, ruined by salt and solitude, as if, from the simple fact that no eyes set upon them, my facial muscles had been subjected to necessities that had nothing to do with expressions; I suddenly feared that I looked only like a gorilla, and my fingers often reinforced this sensation; . . . sometimes, I felt something rigid, tough, sunburned, that even making faces had trouble bringing to life; I must have looked like one of these old cannibal mummies found in vases buried in deserted villages; I was driven into fixed terrors; I thought about this Other that I had pursued for so long, about the disastrous impact I could have caused if God had wished for him to be on this island . . . ; I also thought about this irreversible change of course that could be mine if one day I were truly able to really see myself . . . ;

my anxiety subsided; I took the time to rest, to focus; I went on long, peaceful walks and took time to breathe; I ended up creating the idea of a face; I visualized the details as if I had a real mirror in my cave; my own fingers began to recognize it; the stranger became familiar; I adopted his face; I made it a practice to speak to him, to smile at him and to imagine him smiling back at me; without realizing it, I likely fell into eternal soliloquies wherein I did the questioning and answering, the music and dance . . . but it did not matter, my lord, I finally had a counterpart . . . ;

the day came when I began to consider this imagined face was all but an illusion; I spoke so much with this other self that it had taken shape without needing a face; he was here, there, behind, near, far, all over; present within me as much as by my side, but always in a reassuring complicity; to talk to him, I had progressively raised my voice, with the idea of creating a little bit of distance, so we could better exist for one another, and mutually envision each other; he responded to me at the same volume, but with an inflection that became more and more distinct from mine; the topic of our conversations was first and foremost my history with the island, I recounted everything with great sincerity, without embellishing, describing to him in detail the illusions and fantasies into which I had often fallen; I also explained to him how I perceived the island, how turbulent and unpredictable it was; he asked me for clarification, approved some of my analyses or the little philosophical thoughts about life and death and the solitary life that had become familiar to me . . . ;

to make him even more real, I decided to give him a name; I forced myself not to think of any possible names before the baptism ceremony; it was held at dawn, in a gentle light greeted with much birdsong; the day before—even if I now appreciated the wild bushes that delighted the butterflies so—I had weeded the main square a bit below the kapok tree, trimmed the edging of the fence, cleared up the immediate surroundings for a few cubits; at first light, I dressed in my most beautiful pelts, dug out my hat, opened a parasol; in accordance with my new sobriety, I felt no need to hoist what remained of the flag, or to raise the Constitution on its seashell pedestal, or even to display the laws that had maintained the former orderliness of this place; I wanted to be alone and simple with this other "self"; naked and simple with his other "self"; from then on, by articulating as best I could, I kindly introduced myself, telling him I was called Robinson Crusoe, without stating those tens of titles, appointments, administrative positions, and duties that were once my greatest pride; still in the strictest simplicity, I asked him in return if he could kindly introduce himself; there was silence;

standing under the kapok tree, benevolently observing myself, I waited for him to agree to pronounce his name; hearing nothing back, I walked to my bamboo chair, where my administrative offices and multiple archives were piled, clepsydras, a few decrees and ordinances, and a copy of the Constitution carved on goat leather; as I patiently awaited a response, my eyes fell on the table that logged my days; my mind exploded upon the obvious; try as I might to resist, I was not surprised to feel the other self grab hold of it; he took advantage of the situation to confess to me, with this now familiar voice that rose from my belly: *my name is Sunday;* in fact, my lord, according to my calculations, today was Sunday . . . ;

there was some logic to it; I had always kept Sundays as a day of rest; without imposing any other religion than that of law, order, and civilization on the island, having leisure time was a must; it was not a free day; say, on Sundays, other rituals took over—procedures closer to my sole dignity; I dressed in my goat pelt with properly brushed fur of a sumptuous white; it covered my usual clothes like a ceremonious coat; I abandoned my saber, favoring a thin sword, better adapted for a ceremony than for military endeavors; finally, I took a little walk in the company of my two parrots, my dog whenever he was around, and a few pigeons that I flattered with gluttony by throwing them seeds; I roamed freely, never the same way, but still on my official paths and trails, and that ended with the boulevard of orchids; all along this stroll, I wanted my influence, my work, and my great artwork to be perfectly visible; it was vital that no wild intrusion come disturb this satisfying tranquility that I wanted intact; it went off normally without a hitch: the island at the time seemed to submit to my great order; then, I came back to the cave in time to let the bread dough rise, bake it, take out some cheese from my crates, as well as a sparkling raspberry wine left all week to cool in the gurgling of a spring; when the bread was done, I then placed a moorhen rubbed with spices in the clay oven, brightened with slices of sweet potato, stuffed with dried banana; finally, on the great-table, below the kapok tree, silver, crystal, and porcelain, I had a beautiful lunch ceremony; a dignified feast concluded with noble song, likely brought on by allowing myself to abuse the good raspberry wine; Sundays always ended in the back of the cave, on my bed of soft grass, where I would read a few pages of the strange little book; the rest of the time belonged to meditative reverie, then to snoozing that would catch me by surprise . . . ; now that I think of it, unless there was an alert or catastrophe, it was the only day where I was closest to myself; I took the time to have fun and treat myself, to relish the idea of a productive week, all while being prepared should a week of emergencies and challenges present itself . . . ; I talked a long while to Sunday about my Sundays, explaining to him why he had picked the right name; on the day he was baptized, the bread was delicious, and the moorhen, stuffed with crawfish and chunks of pineapple, something magnificent; I thought the wine was perfect, and we sang together before I showed him, while laughing, the strangeness of my dear little book . . . ;

*

Sunday was a pleasant, albeit unpredictable companion; I had trouble defining him; at times dignified, other times rude, occasionally joyful, sometimes depressed and very sad, very nice or violent . . . ; he often multiplied uncontrollably and occupied several facets at once, impatient, excessive, lustful, lazy or hard-working, courageous or cowardly . . . ; I felt like I was dealing with a gang of clowns, or in any case nothing that could maintain any sort of balance, or nothing by the way—I must admit—that seemed entirely foreign to me . . . he destabilized my mood, influenced me despite myself, making me incapable of knowing what I would become the next day, or how many characters I would set into action during the day . . . ;

*

but then again, after some time, I sensed the danger of creating an Other within myself; I began to talk to myself alone, using several intonations, as I had seen it being performed by

a multitude of mad people; they provoked such fear among
the crew that we ended up expelling them to the main yard, or
shackling them to the bottom of the hold; often, for fear of the
evil eye, the captain changed the ship's course to get rid of them
in some impromptu harbor; the mad people inevitably spoke to
themselves, or rather: they always addressed an infinite number
of people inside themselves; I was extremely scared of that; as
I kept spending time with Sunday deep down inside, I became
inhabited with Mondays, Tuesdays, Wednesdays, Thursdays,
Fridays and co., never identical, truly a gang of eccentrics that
I had trouble containing, even more trouble dispelling from
within; they echoed my speech, dispersed my thoughts, sent me
in all the wrong directions; I began to come unglued, chatting
to myself and calling out to Sunday only to receive no response;
therefore, my lord, I urged myself to get rid of him . . . ;

I erased Sunday's name from my mouth, but gently so he would
not rebel; as soon I could, I weaned myself from imagining him,
of giving him a face, a tone, or a voice; I just compressed him
deep down within myself, only talking to him silently in the
back of my mind; he simply had to be here, right by my side; I
attempted to abolish all distance between him and me, forcing
him rather to be in proximity, to the most intimate parts of my
body and soul; without diminishing the impact of his existence,
it allowed me a better balance and avoided the risk of losing
him for good . . . ;

immediately after, my relationship with the island also changed;
I no longer tried to look around for my former places, to guess
where my old framework lay beneath the invasion of grass; I
made sure to protect my mind from the memories that each
place, gesture, and glance brought back by the dozen; I remained on the fringes of the past, removed even from the things
that currently surrounded me; I entered a field, or I approached
a tree, with a free mind and an empty gaze; at first, I allowed my
ears, skin, hands, tongue, or bare feet the time to feel a change
in sensation and various points of contact, most of which remained undefined and undefinable; I was able to separate
noises, smells, images, colors, and flavors from the center of my

perception . . . , only to keep that sole sensation; insects, sand, heat, trees, flowers, movements or creatures flying, included in this state of consciousness, began to take up residence closely within me, coming, going, merging with the now-silent Sunday; it put me in a mood that had no name in the languages that I remembered; a mood is not an emotion; it exists much more vaguely than other states of being, joy or sadness; feelings occupy our moments of consciousness and affect them in their own way; a mood does not occupy or modify anything as long as it is kept in its natural state, devoid of any condition . . . ; great hermits or other great mystics certainly must have practiced their religion this way: no temples, no churches, no altars, no faces, no images, no emotions, no feelings, just the sensation of a special connection without any boundaries and a source no longer detectable . . . ;

I found myself facing another self: the whole, entire island; I now perceived it like a multitude that touched me, grabbed me, squeezed me all over, as if I were immersed in a mass of presences, imperious and lively; yes, my lord, even if it is difficult to believe: *presences!* . . . ;

distraught, I opened my eyes and let my reason reestablish some order in this chaos; the things around me began to find their exact place and nature; and I, I found . . . my exact solitude; I started to miss everything like a raging fire; I then closed my eyes halfway, stripping myself of the most powerful senses one by one; I moved forward like this, my body free and wide open, bestowing it unto the island winds . . . until the phenomenon occurred once again and carried me away in its stampede; soon, I was able to keep my eyes open, listen, touch, taste, and look without altering this fairyland: the island was an infinite mosaic of *presences* . . . and I had become a hungry messmate;

*

my lord, these *presences* were concentrates of life . . . a plenitude of existence and vitality . . . generally, this is how one feels in front of the deeply moving beauty of a woman or the brilliance of a wonderful child ... ; yet, in my rediscovery of the island, the word had come to me in an ecstatic breath: *presences!* ... ; they emerged everywhere, in the trees, rocks, grass, and imposed the intensity of their sole existence on me almost tangibly ... ; it became impossible for me to understand this phenomenon; such vitalities must have come from a network of contact and exchange, between the ground, air, sand, foam, plants, minerals, without even taking into account animals and insects, and many an invisible thing ... ; each blade of grass, each ancestral tree or lack thereof, each lavish or humble landscape constituted a hosanna of enduring correlations; all thrived, to various degrees, but some of them grew to such completion that they reached a sort of plenitude, and stood out right away from the rest of their peers; one could see them, smell them, hear them, taste them, experience all of them at once and from everywhere, like impalpable units: *presences* ... ! I was so fascinated that I believed they were gifted with intention and movement; I believed I saw the kapok trees go into procession on moonlit nights; I had the pleasure of discovering a display of large silver rocks ... ; and of noticing that certain birds or insects flew by riding the wind to go from *presence* to *presence,* forming small vehicles that transported souls ... ; with this perception (sensation? intuition?), I had become incapable of finding myself before the sea, and of really considering it; a submersion of my consciousness then followed with such a level of intensity that each wonder flooded my mind; I do not know how to say it differently: the sea, my lord, was a colossal *presence* ... ;

*

in these times of *presences,* Sunday took on a troubling consistency; I still had the feeling that he was here, in *contact* as well, but his perception of things was distinctly different from mine: I had no means of accessing it; what he really was to me was no longer conveyed by the intimacy we shared; he was made up of shadows, mysteries, instabilities, of an ambiguous alterity that made him disturbing-alluring, always unpredictable; not only did he constitute an alter ego, but also an unattainable one;

someone asking to be revealed; I eventually told myself that he was also waiting for an . . . Other to blossom; as if my own presence were insufficient to satisfy this expectation . . . ; I had trouble admitting this embarrassing impression, yet it was obvious: Sunday, my other self, became silent, awaiting an Other to fulfill himself that was not me; it was truly unsettling . . . ;

I then believed I understood this abyss that the footprint had opened; I had gone searching for a phantasmic Other, with an infinitely powerful thirst and desire for humanity, yet I had not considered how this Other had at that same moment awakened within me; how much since then, somewhere within me, he also hoped for this Other . . . ; this illusory presence, these fevers and excitement had sent me back to myself, my lord, but with uncertainty as well as fragility; even if this Other inspired by the footprint had existed, that he had materialized at the bend of the shore, the other self, my Sunday, would have come from nowhere at the same time; by way of meeting, I would have had to live, both internally and externally, an outburst of these *presences* . . . ;

sometimes, I told myself that the meeting had taken place; that the footprint had, in its revelry of excitement and illusions, created this unreachable-Other that had allowed me to awaken this Other-deep-down-inside-myself: this Sunday that had begun to live authoritatively; it was fascinating to discover an apparition so intimate; it did not conjure anything distinct from what I knew about myself, but it radiated enough strangeness to force me to consider myself differently, from top to bottom . . . ; anyway, it filled a void, restored a balance, instilled a tinge in the immense greyness; thus the idiot I had become after all these years may have transformed into . . . a small person;

*

through pursuing this unattainable-Other fomented by the footprint, and through desiring him, I had conferred on him the density of an invisible *presence*—as if I had created a new,

contagious, galloping substance that had begun to spread everywhere . . . ; I kept this possibility open, my lord, just to bear
what I was going through . . . ;

*

and consequently, the island before me was no longer threatening, rather an expanse, with neither beginning nor end, where
exchange was possible, and where exchange went strong; one
was shaped in *presence* by the density of relationships that
could be evoked thereof and reverberated around; it would kill,
assault, support, interfere, build on itself, using every possible
change and exchange, as well as their opposites, to remain stable or to prosper . . . ; in these exchanges, there were no good
feelings, or benevolence, love, hate, good or bad, insanity, or
logic, or even some sort of finality; just the greatness of connections; certain *presences*—gigantic rocks, thousand-year-old
trees, venerable turtles, or a dazed bug coming out of meta-
morphosis—were so expertly powerful that they radiated like
the sun; yet, they were located in fluctuating equilibrium where
their survival would certainly play out: their plenitude never
seemed so definitive, and their life expectancy seemed to arise
from a constant rebirth; others were much more discreet, more
fanciful (a duck egg, the nothingness of a ladybug, a mushroom
in velvety moss . . .)—only, by looking at them carefully, I remained stunned by the great vivacity of their exchanges with
everything else, and I was always transported to discover how,
despite their immobility or their supposed withdrawal, they
participated in the overall movement; in all of that, the least
of connections, and therefore the most insignificant, was I, my
lord, it was only I . . . ;

I had come down with a strange fever that drove me to burn the
flag, the island's Constitution, to get rid of the administration,
rules, and regulations; I dunked my last governmental ledger
into the sea until it was soaked, then let it dry and so provide me
with blank pages; on the wall at the back of the cave, I wiped
out all my ancestors; I had drawn them in a series of faceless

portraits, with moustaches, nice hats, ruffs and justaucorps, wigs and scented powder; from then on, they had established a precise line of descent, from a great-grandfather to an imaginary father via a few mothers; these effigies were conveyed by way of ink made of flowers and fish, on panels of tree bark; I had spent some time linking them one by one to most of the objects brought back from the frigate, in such a way that they had begun to compose a perfectly legitimate heritage . . . ; or even: a legacy that finalized this genealogy; I happily cast it aside, as if I were knocking down walls and fences of my former self around the person I had become;

I pushed over the remaining fences around my fields and pasturelands; I opened up paths among thorny hedges that protected my now empty pens; I dismantled fortifications, portcullises, palisades, and the bamboo traps that secured most of the shores . . . ; finally, I was pleased to see my domesticated herds frolic in a highly mobile society, approaching the day as they pleased, no longer respecting any of the idiot's decrees; it was a joy to see them roam, especially as they had internalized an extremely familiar relationship with me, which allowed me access to their milk, sometimes their meat, to heal them whenever necessary, without having to gallop too much; however, there were times when I could not approach them for weeks; there were no longer any dependent, obedient, or submissive relationships between us, just contact as a result of chance or surprise; I was attacked by a young billy goat that I thought to be a friend, so violently that my thigh was bruised for some time; I fell hard under his assault; he stamped around me while belching in anger; it threw me into such a hilarity that he felt abashed; I loved this brutal ardor, the distance that suddenly arose and that brought real freedom; we remained friends-not-friends, by way of head butts, hostile promiscuity, or calm indifference; and I was happy with that;

in these times of *presences,* my lord, it was extraordinary for me to simply see the sun appear—its rays did not fall from the sky: they rose from dark pockets causing all the birds to

awaken and sing; there is so much light in the *presences;* I saw
some spring from the darkest of old tree bark, then dissolve
into the air to make it brighter; I saw some surge from the land
and go on to poke at the stars; after enjoying this show, I led a
life turned juvenile after this contact with the surroundings; my
mind as a small person was capable of eagerly appreciating it
all, without any apprehension or any of this elation that paves
the way for blindness; the animals must have sensed it because
my young billy goat almost never attacked me anymore; when
he did, I made sure to avoid him, but without being surprised
or disappointed by this attack; just like for all the rest, my relationship to the billy goat had to be constructed each day, each
day was unexpected, always unpredictable, never facilitated by
some sort of precedent or a definitive set of ideas; I expected
nothing of him, he expected nothing of me; in this pledge of respect that retained without taking, that offered without giving,
that took away without reducing, we could spend hours next to
each other, and just as many days carefully avoiding each other;
I maintained with each tree, creature, as well as with secluded
places or vast landscapes, relationships whose obvious continuity remained undefinable; it was a delight: I had become the
friend-not-friend of the entire island;

*

the way I hunted had changed; I had put away the muskets and
bullets; I used rudimentary traps that only served me in fair
and useful ways; now forgotten, the exhilaration of shooting
at ortolans flying by! . . . ; now forgotten, these dark frenzies
that drove me to throw away several goats I had killed for no
reason! . . . ; now forgotten, accumulating fruits and vegetables
when I suspected imminent invasion or when I established the
logistics of an imaginary escape on a makeshift raft! . . . ; I was
free because I was freed from all of that; I no longer desired to
own or eat everything; I no longer feared starvation or short-
age; I no longer tried to escape this prison-like place, nor to
transform it into what I thought I had lost; I only opened each
moment to great spaces—not to say, *escape routes* . . . ;

the bamboo pipes built to collect water from springs and bring it close by were redirected; I put them to the service of a group of tortoises, an old tree, a colony of birds, or directed them fully toward drought areas; I had removed the piping in such a way that hundreds of migratory birds came to drink, while the moving water went to utilities foreign to my own subsistence; in the same mind-set, I created a reservoir in the hills and in the waterproof clay area that preserved rainwater as well as what I poured in from the springs; in times of great drought, these reserves now freely flowing supplied thousands of lives; they allowed me to avoid those storage barrels of water full of sediment and more akin to soup; from this point forward, I only drank moving water;

one day, I came across a family of opossums; they belonged to a species I had never seen on this island; this kind of discovery was frequent; seawaters washed up many nonnative creatures on the shores, and they began to proliferate very quickly; this family was complete so to speak, father, mother, children, and even older specimens, probably the patriarchs; I loved the idea of family; I took the big ledger, opened a blank double page, on which I drew not a fictive family tree as I had done many times—I no longer needed a cock and bull story!—but my "geographic tree"; it indicated the places on the island that were dear to me, or that I preferred for one reason or another; rather than naming them in my old possessive-possessing way, I mentioned them with words as vague as *jasmine, wind, dream, pleasure, tenderness, love, kiss* . . . ; then I completed this tree with a bunch of faraway shores, coasts, cities, nations, regions, lands . . . , resurfacing from my lost memories or what had haunted my long Sunday night reveries; then I placed my young billy goat on it, a few orchids, my late dog, parrot-brothers, a grasshopper-cousin, opossums, and a thousand creature-allies, from here or elsewhere, that were part of my affections; while contemplating this tree, I believed I saw a singular country, *my country*, the one where I lived; it consisted of this island but spread well beyond that, in my feelings, my body, my memory, my mind, and realized the relationship of the person I had become with the idea of the island, even with the thought of the world beyond forgetting me;

when I considered it all, this imaginary country was composed so heterogeneously that I felt like I lived on—if not with my body at least with my person—an archipelago measuring the expanse and depth of a continent, which at the same time would have remained lightweight, almost fluid and fluctuating with my states of consciousness and life; this tree that I kept on completing, or modifying, reinforced the idea that I was a network of living connections, which endlessly changed and changed me at the same time, shaping me into a living person; one day, I removed "geographic" and I called it: *tree of life;* from "geographic" emerged the expanse, from "life" the dimension opened;

*

in these times of *presences,* I surprisingly discovered there was no species of insect or animal that would be naturally resistant to doing business with me; no longer submitting to the obsession of hunting or domesticating them, they attracted me with their mysteries, and I attracted them with mine, arguably by what had been transformed within me; for many a night, I was visited by fireflies or green stink bugs constantly landing on my skin and my little book; I had friends-not-friends among the crabs and hermit crabs that were only approachable at night; and on certain days, I walked accompanied by butterflies and small rodents that I took pleasure in not baptizing . . . ;

*

Sunday was still within me, but he remained an enigma: I must have known him, studied him, observed him; what I brought back from him fulfilled me, and reinforced my own salience to the detriment of his; but I kept an active awareness of his presence, like a thousand small paths potentially running deep within me; a thousand escape routes . . . ;

*

in the era of *presences,* I lingered over my strange little book
more and more often; I have not, my lord, until now, mentioned
the link that joined us together, and with good reason: it was a
problematic relationship; yet, the little book was always in one
of the calabashes hanging from my waist, an inseparable companion; I had never really considered it an object, or a book,
but as *something-that-was-there,* with me, without reaching out
for me; distant company, an impossible enigma to unravel that
was kept out of reach; originally, I had caught sight of it among
the fragments of a broken jar, in the section of the steerage that
I could still access; it lay among other books and management
ledgers; I had begun by neglecting all of this, as I was occupied
with carrying barrels of powder, guns, and tools; these trips of
absolute necessity lasted several seasons, before the tide caused
the wreck to be inaccessible; I began plundering it once again
long after, when the frigate became reachable without too much
danger;

this time, I began to search for useful and ornamental objects;
I had brought back brushes, combs, buttons, jewelry, pipes, a
snuffbox, et cetera . . . , piled up in my warehouse at the back
of my cave or visibly arranged for their pleasant aspects; then,
I had distanced myself from the ship, eager to determine if I
was on one of these savage islands used as a stepping stone
for the Americas; I had felt the need to draw the first maps of
the island in order to better find my bearings and to organize
my rescue mission: large pyres, positioned on propitious capes,
easy to light at the slightest hint of a sail; as part of my setting
up, the need for precise maps, and therefore a desk to draw
them on, had sent me back to explore the frigate, notably this
book jar that I could not tear from my mind; I had come back
on the wrong day; the sea was so powerful that it had spit on
to the shore yet more corpses that it had already beaten to a
pulp, eaten by sharks and salt; several of them with shackles
on their ankles and arms that cut into the bone, as if they had
been chained to something underwater since birth; I had taken

out one of my rafts to face the shark-infested swell; their bacchanalia around the frigate had always been fervent, probably because of the rotten corpses that she sowed; the frigate lived its last moments; tipping over on its side, half-broken on the edge of the cays, and disappeared in whirlpools, plank by plank, mesh by mesh; I had managed to get onboard and had begun to search for this broken jar without delay; it was a strange place to put away books; the captain must certainly have wanted to save his writings; the jar had been shattered in the violence of the wreckeyage; its content floated in the fragments that remained on-site; after I had gathered them all, books and ledgers, hastily, in my fiddlewood basket, I had confronted sharks once again, and gotten back to the shore with my ultimate prize; behind me, with a violent crack, the frigate had suddenly dismantled, spilling its guts, spitting other treasures that floated their way to the shore in the foam, through the swell and tide;

*

the two ledgers had faded, along with most of the other works to varying degrees, and their binding had fallen apart; the little book had caught my attention, heavily damaged as well; different from the rest of the books, very thin, just a few pages, and covered in black leather with no title; inside, if my mysterious memory served, were lines of letters in ancient Greek; right away, I thought I was dealing with a poem; water had erased a few pages, by a fourth, half, or a large section of a page; the book of mostly faded double-sided pages consisted of a few Greek phrases and their translation into a language that was accessible to me; I put it out to dry in the sun with the other books; when they had dried, I brought them into the cave, and pressed them under rocks in order to prevent swelling; as soon as I was able to read them, I browsed through them here and there, during my breaks, before sleeping, and often on Sundays during those meditations that served as an epilogue for my long weeks; the ledgers, mostly erased, were merchant books, accounting, stocks, and detailed accounts of all sorts; they also listed other unclear crops from faraway shores; the ink had disappeared or left only an underlying shadow; other books were works of entertainment, likely tales, stories, fables, and romance novels; if reading them was impossible, their images could still be contemplated, since they had resisted the water so well that they had begun to inhabit my mind;

the only books that preserved their print were my precious little book and another work, just as thin but of larger size; they had floated next to one another in the jar, almost identically resistant to water; this coincidence made them twins in my eyes; they could be read in several places, but they only consisted of solitary sentences, obscure verses, strange words, enigmatic expressions, short opaque paragraphs, which related nothing . . . ; these scattered fragments, which made no sense to my feeble understanding, had well suited my brief reading sessions, inspired by boredom or the obligation to maintain mental acuity; over time, feeling my mind drift away, I persistently engaged in it; it was important for my mind to work and reflect upon a few sentences; even though I was insensitive to poetry, I grew to somewhat appreciate reading these remains rescued from the water:

. . . I searched for who I was . . .

. . . one must say and think: also be . . .

throughout the seasons, the books of fables had crumbled; their images had survived only in ghostly reflections; despite my caution, their paper turned to dust between my fingers; no amount of glue or casing could prevent them from ending up in shreds inside the calabash; the little black leather book had valiantly survived; its brother in texture on the other hand had quickly traveled down the path to dust; the idea of losing it became unbearable; to save its fragments, I had copied them on the erased parts of its alter ego; this transfer from one to the other took me several years; letter by letter; word by word; when a paragraph could not fit in a given space, I continued it somewhere else; this task of the copyist had kept me busy secondarily, the urgency reserved for survival work and the incessant plans to escape this trap; the work had ended up disappearing, but I was able to transfer everything that could be saved into the little black book; my inscriptions were placed all over, depending on my mood, and probably due to my mental drifts; they had not been written in the same ink; certain inscriptions had very quickly turned pale, I had to redo them with a thousand other concoctions made from cuttlefish ink and ground rock; often, when one of the pages was in jeopardy, I had cut the fragments to glue them directly into faded spaces of the strange little book: colorful inks, a changing writing style, and makeshift collage had given it the look of a book of spells;

... it is entirely the same ...

... the sun is new every day ...

... as a whole it is filled with life ...

to save my little book, I sheltered it in a special calabash, its cover now waterproofed with beeswax; I washed it regularly with a rag soaked in rum and bitter herbs that killed vermin; the cover was so solid that nothing could break it; even when cyclones swamped the cave with ocean spray, it did not sustain much damage; it dried without a problem; it suffered assaults only from bugs sometimes drilling holes, other times from traces of mold, but nothing that would ever put it in danger; over time, my inks had remained stable, and could be read easily, even in the glimmer of my piteous candles; as a precaution, I often reinforced the upstrokes and downstrokes, which allowed me to better memorize the words, sentences, and phrases that I repeated during my sessions or when I used them for signs and other proclamations of solitary emperor;

... the way for the Word, there only remains: there is ...

... if you do not hope, you will not find what was unhoped for, without it all is unobtainable, and a dead end ...

over the years, the little book had become extremely precious to me; I had come out of this mental exercise, to throw its words to be carried by the wind or make them echo in the rumbling acoustics of the caves; I had found pleasure in this, childish, playful, loud, and unnecessary; I had thus changed my perception of printed things; for me, writing had always been about adding and subtracting, ledgers and registrations useful to ship-owners in order to keep track of their business; I must have been rather a man of action; and if I knew how to read-and-write as well as I did, it certainly must not have been my main job or my favorite task—yet this became the case in this eternal exile;

FIRST VOICE
. . . the same him is both thinking and being . . .

SECOND VOICE
. . . awake, they sleep . . .

I had started to hear two voices, two whispers, two sighs, and two distinct intonations while reading it; these fragments maintained the resonance of two people that I ended up differentiating without any hesitation; they were consciousnesses without bodies or faces, of an infinite sensitivity, both tormented and imbued with tranquility; coming from olden times, these voices continued to live in quiet authority, friend of wisdom;

FIRST VOICE
. . . it is entirely about where I begin,
for once again I shall return . . .

SECOND VOICE
. . . but one must remember the person who forgets where
the path leads . . .

I had no idea if these voices knew each other, if during their time they had met, or to what extent they had spoken, answered, or argued with one another, but they had seemingly practiced this exchange in this forced connection at the heart of the little book; I knew they were strangers to my preoccupation; at the same time, what I had experienced day after day in this irreversible exile had sent me back close to them; their dark, shadowy experiences were simply handed to me, offered but never at my disposal; these experiences had enlightened me with their obscurity; cast shadows over their secret insight; allowed me to somehow resist these mental storms that I had endured over the course of my harsh solitude;

FIRST VOICE

. . . what is necessary is this: to say and think of the being as Being: *indeed it is Being, the non-Being on the contrary is not: here is what I invite you to consider . . .*

but of both voices, the most enigmatic, determined, and the roughest tone emerged from the original fragments of the little book itself; I had called it the poem of poems, *inaugural poem,* the one that created my portable library with two voices; it was the only one whose name I had guessed from one of the flyleaf pages, also nearly erased; at the beginning, an author's name did not matter to me at all; I was just looking for words and sentences to preserve my voice and keep my mind occupied; when the voice had risen, powerful and singular, I had desired to make its acquaintance, and of course to give it a name; I was then able to rewrite the printed letters tracing them dot by dot, and reinforcing them by the tip of my eagle-feather quill; the man must have been called *Parmenides,* or *Parmeniles;* I had remained hesitant between these two possibilities for a long time, then I settled on "Parmenides"; for reasons unclear, this name suited the voice that I heard rising from the printed extracts; the other voice, copied by my hand, much more fluid and spry, turned its back on the other individual, or strived to resist him; in any case, it seemed like the second voice had always heard the first and had begun to move with him being ever attentive . . . ;

FIRST VOICE

. . . admittedly, it is not a tragic fate that put you on this road (because it is well away from the path of humans), but justice and law . . . yet one must be educated in all things,

of the heart of truth without trembling, consummate sphere,
but also of what mortals have in sight,
where nothing true is to be trusted . . .

SECOND VOICE
. . . the awoken people have but one world,
but sleeping people each have a world of their own . . .

I had sanctified the little book a thousand different ways; first, by reading it each night just before my tormented sleep; then, at dawn ceremonies, or during my meager morning intake, I had monotonously read fragments of it; other times, I had placed it in front of me, contemplating its uncompromising darkness, convinced I was in front of a real library; I was fascinated that two great distinctive voices along with so many words and images were able to fit in so little space; in my delirium, I had built a house of worship where I could exhibit it like a host of high humanity; during a beautiful ceremony, I placed the book on an altar located at the back of my cave, next to the ancestors' effigies, "family" objects, and a mess of small symbols that installed me as master for each of these pieces of land; covered in sumptuous pelts, I sometimes carried it across the island, holding it at arm's length and stating a few snippets every twenty feet; back at the cave, I returned it to its house of worship and greeted it like a divine friend; my mind had always been variable: such a worshipped object could fall from grace in no time; the book had crossed the craziest times all the while remaining something special, distant yet necessary for my mind which it endlessly intrigued; during less reverent times, however much I transcribed these fragments onto cave walls, engraved them on gum tree bark, drawn a thousand signs and just as many inscriptions out of it, the little book had remained this opaque little block, radiating a wild beauty that called me back to it at the slightest separation; it truly was a solidity that I used to prop myself up in order to remain standing;

FIRST VOICE
. . . the daughters of the Sun, who had abandoned
the palaces of the Night,

ran toward the light while in my procession,
their hands moving aside the veils that concealed their heads . . .

SECOND VOICE
. . . to live from death, to die from life . . .

the idiot that I was had too often grappled with the idea of
"understanding," of deciphering the fragments word for word
that scattered across faded pages; the little book had always
resisted these "explanations"; however much the idiot had repeated them to himself, meditated on them during his work as
founding master, involved parts of the text in his great works of
construction—even more thrilling for him that the Greeks were
the soul of the old frigate, that they were at the basis of the very
idea of civilization—upon his return, he fell right back to that
block positioned there, which stared at him, more impenetrable
than a moonless night, murmuring its secret lives and mysteries;

*

I avidly began reading again during this time when I felt I was
surrounded by *presences;* without really knowing why, feeling
in harmony with my surroundings, I wanted to find the little
book a place, especially to determine what it could add to this
new endeavor; probably also because its voices now appeared
as two tangible *presences,* just as fabulous as the ones surrounding me all the time; I began to read again with this new
sensitivity that I felt transforming me; I proceeded differently:
silently reading a portion, then quietly, then loudly, then repeating it endlessly in various lively tones, with the idea that a faster
reading would grasp the meaning like a hunter ferrets a hare
out of the woods; not the slightest opening; total opacity; I even
felt like it had strengthened; each fragment remained a small
obscure block that no longer even concerned me, but it seemingly frolicked in the continuous quivering of the grass and the
tall trees; each fragment was there, vibrating in a singular tone,
like an insect soon to metamorphose, and creating a chaotic and
troubling grandeur in its relationship with others;

FIRST VOICE
... there is no beginning nor end,
since generation and destruction have been pushed far away ...

SECOND VOICE
... nothing is permanent, except change ...

despite everything, I read and reread it once more, leaving all attempts at "understanding" aside, just experiencing the rhythm, its sensations and colors, and letting them live in me through the connections I endlessly developed with the living things surrounding me; I felt the little book's *presence*, both singular and dual; the little book was here, with me—not only because it represented an object (small, compact, black) but because of its place in the cavities of my head where it had so often resonated, in my chest where it had rumbled over all these years; its *presence* spread so extraordinarily in concert with those that made up the whole island; one morning I closed it, then holding it at arm's length above my head, from memory I began to proclaim each of the fragments that I now had a perfect knowledge of;

delivering my body and soul into this proclamation, I felt how attentive the island was to the book; the fragments in their continuity reinforced the island's lines, crests, density, depth, and expanse; each fragment succeeded in revealing the island as a vast *presence* too, protean and composite; I soon felt the dynamic of powerful energies laid before me, turning around me, passing through me; the fragments spread in this mosaic with incredible ease, filled the cracks like glue, or like the substance of invisible cement; their strangeness was in perfect harmony with the reality that undulated around me; in this proclamation, my voice itself had changed, I no longer recognized the timbre: the words of the little book materialized in an internal beat as autonomous beings; they inscribed their resonance in a beam of connections that banded the whole island together in a ring of strength around my body; this was the strange part: *I perceived the island in a new and extremely moving totality;* each of the *presences* contained the quintessence of a totality vaster than they were; the island began nowhere, did not spread in any certain direction, seemed whole within each of the *presences,* and equally as far beyond; the island was bestowed upon me in an incredible flamboyance, happily revealed by the words of the little book; I then remembered the pearls found in the flesh of large oysters; it was said that they originally formed from a wound: grains of sand which had crept their way into their shells, or which certain savages had inserted into them, and which these animals neutralized over the years in a prison of mother-of-pearl; I did not know if this island had a similar intent for me—*pain and wound transformed into beauty;* what was certain is that the island enveloped me as she did each fragment I brushed against; in my vanity, I had thought that it was I who projected a thousand connections toward the island, but in return I detected such a hold over me that it was obvious the island was attached to me, and had mercilessly swallowed me; I felt my heart derail; then I resigned myself to the idea of being a pearl in the island's body; perhaps it was the price to pay to also become a *presence* in concert with the others . . . ;

so, I proclaimed the fragments with even more joy, strength, and love, more *hope,* too; I gave them to the island as acceptance of what it would make of me; there was no need to convince me, I said over and over again that it was a living organism, not a desert island; not a hostile prison but life that managed to pull itself from soulless lava; that it was able to attract birds and millions of creatures, use the wind, dirt, pollen, fully exploiting what the ocean had continuously brought over thousands of years, and to accept them into its tremendous mosaic of *presences* . . . ; I was brought to the island as naked as the most insignificant toad, whichever fruit, plant, neither more nor less than it all, and the island would do whatever it wanted with me; the idiot must certainly have felt this vigorous suction; he had deployed his crude artifices against this fear of being swallowed; as for me, I warded it off while accepting it all the same, proclaiming the fragments of the little book urbi et orbi: praying that it would form the substance of my mother-of-pearl;

FIRST VOICE
. . . unconceived he is also enduring; he was indeed
of an intact frame, unwavering and everlasting;
never was he nor will he be, since he now is,
completely whole at once, of a sole outcome;
what generation can we seek for him?

SECOND VOICE
. . . one cannot step into the same river twice;

as I wandered along shouting book fragments, I took down
what was left of the signs, the tatters of pompous naming; I
threw away the remnants of the pipe system; no last bastion
should come between this island and me; I wholeheartedly offered the island all I was, eager to become, eager for this future
the island would impose upon me with an imperious cover; I
uttered the fragments to the birds, to the goats, to the roots; I
hummed them atop the headlands; to wherever the wind blew,
I uttered them on long breaths to watch them take flight like
eagles; at night, I fell asleep jabbering them, and awoke foam-
ing at the mouth still babbling them . . . ; this trance could have
lasted over centuries had the island not suddenly electrified . . . ;

*

at first, there was great silence for a split second; then the ground
began to quake, the trees moving just like a crowd would have;
the birds had disappeared; not a creature moved in the nearby
surroundings; a wild undulation of everything that was fixed
submerged my astounded mind; dragons banged against the
rocks and deep roots;

the island had decided to swallow me whole; I was thrust to
the ground; a rumble suddenly arose from the earth in ebullient
breaths; the ground swayed, abruptly tore, throwing ghostly
hair that floated like mist before falling like burning peat; an
eternity in dire straits continued birthing itself; in utter terror,
I remained on the ground where I had fallen, perceiving faint

cracks, panicked collapses, screeching rocks launched toward the surface . . . ; the ground shook like this for a thousand years, when all of a sudden it stopped;

I stopped moving as well; my eyes squeezed shut; tight tight tight; my body tensed for fear that the island would resume; unknown smells swirled idly about; warm breezes spun in all directions; my apprehension grew stronger; the island had transformed as some caterpillars do; an unknown entity stood above me in a most terrifying reality; I closed my eyes even tighter and remained motionless to avoid being devoured; night soon fell; I had to sleep, my distraught eyes glued to the wall of my eyelids; the morning light fell delicately on my decidedly hypersensitive skin, but no song accompanied the sun; the strange silence was present more than ever; frightening; weightless; no distance or echo; no possible future; tormented by this despair, I remained like this for a couple of hours before daring to slightly open my eyes;

everything lay in an atrocious wreckage: the trees tormented; my cave halfway collapsed; my kapok tree leaning . . . ; spectacular transformations had distorted the landscape around me; nothing was in the right spot; nothing was in place; I felt imbalanced; ties and bearings loose, I gave up on the idea of standing and chose to crawl like a desperate animal in a shifting swamp; my connections with the *presences* had disappeared; incidentally, I could no longer isolate them; I perceived nothing, save for a collection of absences that had sunk like sea wreckage; I was alone; overwhelmed by solitude and burned wood, at the heart of a "thing" that surrounded me without song, noise, hues or smells, or depth either; a flat, strange reality similar to a looted grave, on which I began to sob from distress; my lord, the island had turned into well beyond the worst disenchantment . . . ;

Captain's Log

September 2—In the year of our Lord 1659—These last few days, we sailed alongside two or three islands, without much certainty as to whether we were really headed in the right direction. There are so many! The threat posed by the cays is so poorly indicated on available maps that very few apprentices dare cross these waters. This area had a bad reputation in the great Companies. In my youth, I had been forced to venture there, and I had done it before with skill that is occasionally driven by madness. With the sail shortened and taking constant soundings, I made sure to stick to the coordinates we had followed in the past and that were successful at the time. The worried apprentice looked up at me with widening eyes, and I smiled back to let him know how I was accustomed to following my lucky star.

September 4—In the year of our Lord 1659—In the early morning, we had found the island without any trouble. I could examine the shore with my spyglass. Nothing looks more like an island than another island. Peaks. Cliffs trickling with green. Screeching monkeys. The din of birds that barely held a candle to ancestral silence. A green, dark mass, oftentimes secretive and threatening like the scales of a monster . . . Emptiness . . . Absence . . . Soulless vitality . . . No trace of human life, nothing to indicate that a band of savages had ever passed through. Yet it was still the island . . . except empty . . .

I was disappointed, but something told me to insist. These intuitions, absurd at first glance, had always provided me with unpredictable benefits. Intuition often leads to reality's secrets. To the great displeasure of the apprentice, I gave the order to increase the number of soundings, to double the observers in the matter of the cays, and to maneuver around the island, in hopes of locating the small cove where the event had occurred . . .

September 4—In the year of our Lord 1659—The crew wonders what I am doing . . . It would take so long to explain . . .

3

THE ARTIST

there were several days of silence and odd quietness; the most common creatures had disappeared; instead, I saw little wiggling critters come hurtling with a thousand legs, which forced me to crawl maniacally, I vividly remembered the burning sensation of their venom; I also encountered many lizards with dead eyes, fuzzy spiders extremely fearful of light, and lots of snakes whose glassy scales seemed softened . . . ; this throng which was supposed to languish in the darkness of the soil was now in distress as the sun blazed; in fact, I saw some spring from cracks and craters that formed when the gigantic trees toppled; these monsters lay quartered, in piles of foliage, exposing an indecency of pale roots and tears of sap; I saw the scurrying swarms of ants, among countless creatures that were seemingly made of humus and small anxieties; I crawled arbitrarily, trying my hardest to run from something whose location or motive I did not know, to such an extent that each step brought me as close as it should have been far; danger followed me all around; I was incapable of thinking; incapable of stopping my ears from ringing; incapable of controlling my cheeks from twitching; the shock had been so severe, so much abnormality had occurred at once, and excessively, that restored stability remained an enigma; it took me two or three suns to stand up again; and almost as many to regain a semblance of balance;

I barely recognized the places that I had administered for so long; my goats, hens, and parrots had dispersed all over; I found some shivering inside busted tree trunks, listless in narrow gullies, trembling in entangled bushes; all seemingly awaiting a sign of some sort before trying to resume normal life; an increasing scarcity of life allowed them to breathe, but only with shallow gasps out and hiccups in; especially since the ground could not stop quaking or spasming, which caused a moment of panic each time; in my shaken state, things could not settle where they should; now that I had witnessed the earth cart trees around, the soil become like water, all immobility seemed suspect; the grass concealed dragon vertebrae ready to coil; I suspected the hills of being skulls of gorgons buried under a skin of rocks, looking out for when to emerge hissing; so I proceeded as if each grain of sand were a set of jaws, treading with the greatest care, and ready to immediately throw myself to the ground at the slightest tremble; bugs moved as I did; birds, no doubt wary of the sky, hopped from one shadow to the next as if in anticipation of the entire island invisibly leaping . . . ; days went by like this, more quickly than nights because the latter only deepened the pain; I slept in the middle of an open field, away from the trees, or any cliff capable of holding back hordes of minotaurs; I angled my arms and legs so as not to be swallowed by an unexpected sinkhole; I would even go as far as to harness myself to little shrubs, in order to resist the mouth of the ground should it suddenly appear;

*

this impression of devastation lasted for a long time; I became so greatly accustomed to it that I no longer remembered the island from before the earthquake; rains washed; the sun dried; water brought springs and rivers to life, resuscitated the wounded ground; light poured its invisible benefits; germination occurred all over, extremely intense and hysterical, which could be seen everywhere; an infinity of sprouts emerged where big trees had fallen and even the small trees, now freed from their hold, hurried to grow toward the sky in a flurry; flowers also came back in abnormal abundance, as if they rushed to fill the emptiness and wounds with the substance of their own existence; I began to realize that birds had started flying and singing again, that amorous frenzies emulsified flowers and bunches of fruits, and that every single branch capable of sustaining life outside the reach of predators was weighed down by nests, cocoons, war chants, and territorial refrains;

they were not the only ones searching for rebirth; I did the same, but rather than crowd a territory, I continued this rebirth within me; my quest became attached to this recent euphoria— this blessing that had closely connected me to the tiniest blade of grass, rewarding me with the immeasurable satisfaction that children know; but here, as I strolled along in distress, I found that I was disappointed deep down, and devoid of any drive; my bones had become more visible; my chest mustered only a bestial breath; no longer was my heart attached to or in harmony with anything, and it beat like the flapping of a taut sail; as for my skull, my lord, it only harbored stupefaction that consumed my thoughts one by one; it was unbearable to no longer feel this special relationship that I had experienced so strongly; through artificial images and coerced emotions, I tried to reinstall these *presences* within me; it made no difference; the new germination of the island, so remarkable, did not return this mysterious effect to me of when I had felt a *presence* both singular and multiple, enveloping me as it spread; were something to emerge trembling, it would only be devoured by absence—a heavy, defunct, viscous contagion like an inert land; despite the beauty of the flowers, the proliferation of fruits, the magic of swarms, the plentiful flight of birds, and despite the solemnity of old surviving trees, I remained outside of it all, drifting along, floating toward nowhere, in a void that did not inspire any particular emotion, feeling, or source capable of bringing my mind back to life;

*

it is in this state that I found my way back to the beach of beginnings, the place where I had discovered the footprint; I have no idea why I had come back here; perhaps I was headed toward another beginning and needed to reach this point of origin; it is strange how essential the origin is when one needs to be reborn and begin everything anew as it were . . . ; *what is this mystery behind the place of beginning that never makes it outdated?* . . . ; of course, my lord, this essential question would only come to me long after; when I ventured into the area of the footprint, I was not in this state of mind; in fact, I was in no

state of mind whatsoever; I simply proceeded forward; I had no
expectations; the beach had been devastated; after the quake,
an unbridled wave must have struck the shore with all its might;
greenish remains of the frigate emerged from the foam and
sand; shinbones exhumed from the depths sparkled white in the
glaring sun; algae had risen from the abyss; thousands of fish,
crabs, and seashells rotted all together in an unbearable stench;
I contemplated this desolation without emotion, without dis-
comfort, my mind remaining so still; nevertheless, it was with
heartache that my attention was drawn toward a precise spot;
as I stepped closer, under a blanket of seaweed and spiny lobster
scales, I began to sense a familiar shape; I quickly cleared it with
my foot and recognized the footprint; it was not supposed to
be here, yet there it was; my mind did not contest this absurdity
whatsoever: the footprint was here, intact: I had not damaged
it, nor erased it from the surface of the world;

I remained frozen for a long time before kneeling down and
completely freeing the footprint; with unhurried placidity, I lay
next to it like a worshipper upon seeing an altar; it was indeed
the footprint, still molded in the hardened clay now somehow
mummified; during my lively reaction, I must have displaced
a crust of sand that had stuck to its ridge; the crust had since
gone, leaving it rawly exposed; the initial shape remained imprisoned in the old clay, now fully revealed by the great wave
that swept the shore after the quake; the clay was now bluish,
ribbed with very thin yellow veins, and spotted with some dark
substance similar to potter's clay; most surprising was that the
footprint seemed foreign to me; I myself had not changed, yet
it did not look like the one I had observed for so long, and of
which I kept an ardent memory; here it was, bare, distant, perhaps cold, and most certainly inert;

I looked at it from all directions, lying to its left, contorting
myself to its right, sitting astride it, my arms planted on either
side to stare at it from above; I ended up sitting in front of it
so as to set my foot in it; which I did with no problem; my
foot fit into it once again; and I remained like this, motionless,

attentive, as if I expected it to come to life and wrap around my
ankle; of course, nothing happened; I felt the clay hold in place
under the trembling skin of my foot, stiff, warm on the surface
and cooler in the hollow, it did not resonate, dead as a rock a
thousand times over, fired and baked by the sun and the ages;
I remained like this, with no particular excitement, no grue-
some emotion, either; I pressed my chest to my bent knee and
wrapped my arms around it to lean forward, and I continued
to contemplate my foot that fit into the shape; it is then that the
distortions occurred . . . ;

observing all of that up close, I realized that my heel, the arch of
my foot, and my toes did not fit the footprint quite so snugly; in
many areas, the clay lines diverted from it; in others, they disappeared under my trembling foot; there was room under the arch
of my foot; the presumed toe indentations were much bigger
than my own; a chain of infinite shifts accumulated in my consciousness, leading me to accept that not only was this footprint
not mine, but it could originate from various contingencies; its
connection to the arch of a foot, a heel, and toes was actually
just one possibility among many that my mind had hastily ruled
out; and the worst is that now subjected to my clear lucidity, it
could very well have been inhuman;

*

I remained lying there for several days without moving; perceiving only the fixed footprint, motionless in the ground, lifeless,
without any definitive shape; this emptiness of my being before
it, and this emptiness which rose from it filled me with infinite
unease; I tried to imagine a fabled sea monster coming out of
the water, treading on this beach during a storm, and leaving
this track in the muddy clay; I also imagined the shock of one
of those shooting stars that sometimes fall from the sky, which
would have struck here, so I began to scrape away four cubits of
sand in an attempt to uncover proof of a celestial shower . . . ;
but this pathetic agitation did not affect my body or even spread
to the heart of my mind; *I watched myself become agitated;*

from a distance, I discovered a too familiar fear waken inside me, and I tried hard to respond to it with the same familiarity: I wanted to impose emotional meaning onto this thing in the clay; I could not stand seeing it like this, lifeless, with no influence, with nothing that concerned me, and my mind tried hard once again to cover it with layers of illusions; such a malaise was so uncomfortable for me that at certain abrupt moments I tried to create gods to explain the origin of that thing, and a thousand little demons to make it move; I went as far as to search for primary hallucinations that I wanted to inhabit, from which I wanted to be delivered outright, for the sole purpose of conferring life upon this thing; but I ended up giving this nonsense up and throwing these devices against failure overboard, to be found naked, next to the footprint, observing it with some reservation as if examining the unknown, with the same vertigo and the same confusion . . . ; after an indefinite period of time, I suddenly stood up and left, shambling toward the devastated island;

*

I remained imprisoned in this feeling of malaise, engaging in activities that had always sustained life; cleaning the rust off a tool; greasing an arquebus; using the sun to bring a powder residue back to life . . . ; I set off about these automatic tasks feigning enthusiasm, jumping from chore to chore, without establishing the slightest link between them, without ever completing any of them, nor most importantly managing to be interested in them; everything was done with a hopelessness that showered the simplest desires in absurdity . . . ; in spite of that, I found many tasks to keep myself occupied; the deepest part of my cave had collapsed; my bamboo props had given way at different lengths, and the place, riddled with small cracks, was no longer safe; in a mournful sluggishness, I collected the bare necessities from my old treasures; then, half-hearted still, I visited a few storage caves with the intention of finding alternative lodging; my mind was so cloudy that I made do with one simple cave; one by one, I indifferently brought objects over from my main cave, leaving most of them behind, as they seemed so incongruous each time; I arranged the poor cave as much as I could, and I left as soon as night fell: it was now impossible to find sleep under a roof of any kind;

my first conscious night after the quake was, to say the least, strange; in the bizarre silence only the roar of the sea remained perceptible; I sensed the waves disperse coral, take cliffs away, eat at mangroves, dig, dig everywhere; the ocean wanted to sink the island into the torn abysses below; I thought the ground was crumbling under my weight, but this impression quickly vanished; it was only an illusion; my mind struggled like this; my back on the ground, I stared at the celestial ceiling; instead of a delightful spectacle, I experienced, my lord, the blow of an obscure infinity, flecked with immemorial brilliance, in an indifference so deprived of will that it led me to a latent fear; relentless mystery lay in the place where I had always touched divine harmony: a thing without existence, before all existence, and beyond the reach of anything possible; plunged into stupor, I remained in front of it, eyes widened, fixed, without thinking, my only anchor being the trembling of my body: excessiveness flooded from the sky, excavated the rumbles of the sea, and filled the island and my mind at the same time with an irreversible *shock;* my lord, please forgive this tear, but this shock was difficult to endure;

*

this became my usual feeling of malaise; I paid no mind to the animals who were once my pets in need of my care; I ignored the parrots to whom I had taught a couple of swear words and who, while echoing them, pursued me; I was dissolved in a lucidity similar to a wound—but a wound stripped of consistency or pain; I could remain still for hours looking at an insignificant tree, taking in the atmosphere of a gully, or searching for the wind that usually recounts so many things; now, it no longer said much of anything; the wind was not even the wind anymore: just the release of nothing that went nowhere;

this self-focused lucidity allowed me to understand the extent to which that idiot, then that small person I had become, had concealed these lives and realities with artifice; I had not stopped making the island over and over in my head; my mind had taken on the unending task of concealing the island under the veil of my illusions, maintaining a false equilibrium; there, in my halting lucidity, I perceived nothing other than what I saw; I could see pairs of armadillos with red eyes pass by and found no purpose for them; or contemplate blue crabs filing by without imagining they would change shelters; the flight of a magnificent frigate bird or even the inconsistencies of the sky failed to inspire me to trace out the steps of an imaginary polka; a binding lucidity made me a stranger to all of that, incapable of the slightest complicity or proximity, and not at all affected in the slightest by anything; I was extremely frightened by it all, my lord, extremely frightened: *was it this dark melancholy that unhinged sailors? . . .*—but I felt no sadness within me; I fell asleep smoothly; woke up apathetic; revisited no memories, or any future; I engulfed my days in routines that did not even make use of one-fourth of my mind; my days began aimlessly, and ended unfulfilled; my slow, diligent gestures seemed to have never known any passionate inspiration; it was even more alarming that the island had never been as flowery, as generous in fruits, vegetables, insects, or as diverse in birds and animals . . . ;

such a glorious abundance of life kept calling my attention; I looked at it all without greed, in an absence that worsened my now permanent malaise; I saw the long wounds of the ground fill with greenery; the fallen gum trees stand up again on their own, or grow new branches from their sides; their old bark exploded in buds; I looked at nests of red bugs thrive, endlessly busy with building something invisible, their bustling only generating more bustling; I observed groups of migratory plovers descend upon the island for a few hours before leaving with the wind for the horizon; I had long been fascinated by migratory birds; they knew what lay beyond; they were not prisoners of any sort of boundary; I had always seen them arrive with

elation as if they were confirming the existence of a world beyond this prison-like island; to see them go away had repeat-
edly thrown me into dismay as I let out an envious sigh; sons of
the winds, friends with great spaces, so mobile, so light, so far
from this stump to which the island had reduced me! ...; their
life seemed to me a fully achieved mode of existence, probably
the finest way to live out one's existence; but now, these sudden takeoffs, spreading enthusiastically, swirling with vitality,
seemed to me like a freedom that came from neither hell nor
paradise, but rather from nothing, and for nothing; just here,
intense, vibrant, immeasurable, indifferent toward anything in
particular, and lacking the will to achieve; I simply watched
them, without desire, without disgust;

the most pathetic were the remains of my illusory splendor:
signs, animal pens, stores, various fortifications, pompous main
squares, avenues and trading posts ...; only erased lines subsisted under the alliance of bushes and unleashed animals; the
fields of wheat and barley of which I was once proud were now
competing with overgrown plants, they must have changed in
nature or diverted to another existence; I had saved some grains,
planning, idealistically, to replant them, but to see them in the
palm of my hand did not awaken anything in me, no vision of
flour or scent of warm bread, or the possibility of fermented
beverages; nothing; just obtuse grains, subjected to a fatality of
which they were unaware, that sparked no interest in my mind;
the rats and cats that had worried me for so long now belonged
to a natural profusion whose abundance and specificity came
to me without distinction, with the same relevance and scope;

*

facing this situation, my mind always tried to create alternatives for survival; but what I developed in an emotional outburst never became meaningful for my hollowed-out senses;
one day, at dawn, I stumbled upon a quivering mass of small,
geometric figures stuck together, their edges dissipating as the
wind blew; this round form sat on top of a protuberance, thick

and red, that leaped twisting from the ground while bearing the weight of the quivering mass; the little things were radiating with what they took from the light, just darkened in certain spots by intense shade; it resembled nothing I had ever known; I felt extremely uneasy in front of this apparition, and wanted to persuade myself that it was an old mango tree—an old tree, long-standing friend—that had been one of the *presences* with which I'd felt a connection; I talked to it, named it, touched it, alas! . . . the impassive oddity got the upper hand, pushed me away though with no ill will, and stared at me with little interest; these inhalations of light, the energy that I sensed flowing from the ground to inhabit this thing and spread through it imperceptibly, standing before me while having no effect; I was caught in a nudity of appearances that my mind could not control, or even interpret in any way; wherever I looked, everything was made of the same thing around me . . . ; it is only then that I felt like I existed on this island; in this unknown contact that consisted of no real encounters; what existed with as much intensity were no longer figurines of my mental theater, nor even the docile deviations of my human nature; I did not know what it was, but now the human no longer existed, it was no longer able to put a system in order, to bring about any consistency; no nature, no landscape, no living thing, no humanity stationed in an ivory tower: only somewhat scattered hints of perception, part of a long, static indecipherability . . . ;

the objects that had so closely surrounded my survival seemed disanimated; their substance was lost in the memory of the frigate; axes, pickaxes, saws, chisels, triangles, and pincers . . . emerged from here and there, like ghosts, as unidentifiable as the mushy corpses washed ashore had been; the weapons had the same effect on me; I who had never set foot outside without a musket strapped to my shoulder now abandoned them to rust, wear and tear, and no longer contemplated using them for anything; my fingers alone sufficed to feed me; I had become skilled in trapping birds with my hands, catching young muskrats, or hooking the silver-gilt ear of a sleepy shark with my forefinger; animals no longer perceived me as a possible threat; they approached me in clear indifference; I had become as natural as the great trees, as ardent as the flowers, as swaying as the razor grass; it is also true that my eyes presumed nothing about them; yet no morbid stupefaction struck me: only an abrupt perception from which the entire island emerged, in its infinite detail, the magnitude of its entirety, right in the center of my consciousness yet outside the reach of my mind;

*

the gigantic listless emergence that constituted this island tossed me between fits of nausea and malaise; when I was not thinking about it, and was able to rest my soul, it led me toward a slow inner realization, just as what I saw around me did; then I was relieved, in a state that I could not control and that, at worst, I did not perceive; but the relief did not last long, distress, then great malaise, overcame me; this island that was simply here, and that my mind could not shake this pipe dream, provoked within me an irrepressible urge to run away to anywhere, to create a path of detachment that my mind, which had alas slipped further and further away, could no longer offer me; only a great deal of anguish then remained; *anguish,* my lord, *anguish!* ... ; I had chosen this term without much thought—indeed, it reflected the oppression that I felt in my chest—but over the seasons, I was able to identify it more clearly;

what I called "anguish" was not the opposite of joy, was not associated with sadness, and did not emerge from a wound: a lucidity without triumph, a perspicacity without outlets—let's say *a raw availability,* deprived of all illusion, free from emotion; my anguish was content with eliminating every possibility, freezing every fervent desire, and by the same token became unlivable; let's say *impractical* for whoever remains alive; yet, I was alive; I saw, I moved, I perceived the surroundings, *all I could do was continue to live* in this clear and open space; the alternatives were these: either I remained stupefied, becoming stale and rancid in anxiety, or I used that stupefaction to continue living without illusions and chimera; my soul therefore became tightly restricted to a tiny movement that yet remained imperceptible to me for a long time, as if rooted in this inaugural anguish; this is why I gradually rediscovered my will to make, to create freely, and to act in the freedom of this simplicity; the spur to achieve it came from my small traveling library—this little book that had lived through my despair and mental tumult;

*

during these latest events, I had incessantly kept it near me in the safety of a calabash; as for the little book, my new mind-set had changed nothing; it kept its imperious distance; when my indolent wandering brought me back to the outskirts of my new dwelling, I picked it up again as often as I could, during my frightening nights on watch; now, I read it in utter silence; the little book had grown old, its yellowed pages gave unpredictable nuances to the colors of my inks; I no longer had need for it, I wanted no use for it; to hold it, or thumb through it was only a habit to mitigate my anguish; it is perhaps then that my little book began a subtle transformation;

SECOND VOICE
. . . Good and evil are one . . .

until then, I had not understood anything about the little book and had fed on this lack of comprehension; I had even considered that once and for all there was nothing to understand, which allowed me to adapt it to the ebb and flow of my illusions; understanding nothing about these fragments made me use them in more or less mad ways; in this manner, I had avoided them, remaining closely tied to them; when they did not cause anger and irritation, the fragments had always triggered landscapes, fairy tales, images, and little stories within me that had titillated my enchantment; this failure to understand had caused me to invent a thousand diversions so pleasant that I sought to repeat them; the failure to understand remaining absolute, the same words and verses had allowed for endless new tales, and new images, and hours of reading that remained endless as well; a spiral with no way out;

but now, my lord, by reading these fragments over and over again, in this bareness in which my mind had become cornered, something initiated a movement; the printed stanzas of this old Parmenides, but even more so the verses I had copied, began to deviate into undefinable possibilities; I no longer heard these two voices of old motionless wise men which had concocted in the theater of my mind, but two tones that completed each other in a sort of union, and that together produced a new sound; I no longer filled their sentences with these mental images that opened onto long meditative impasses; my eyes caught words, dry, bare, even rough; my unmoving mind inhaled these fragments one by one; they fell into me, like in a resonating cave where together they made sense, with no time to process them; I then reread them, inhaled them once again, and they entered me, blind, blinded, inconsistent, in a circle of meaningless possibilities; only the void of my mind spread toward them, and those equally neutral words bounded toward me; and the place of our encounters remained a space devoid of all shape, language, image, or narrative; and, in my perception, this eternal encounter left no more tracks than a goat hoof on a crust of dry rock; but it subsisted within me like a place of *articulation* where . . . a movement was created—a burst of freshness;

SECOND VOICE
. . . the most beautiful arrangement
is also similar to a pile of trash
collected at random . . .

actually, until then, I had seen the island framed through my mind, and not only had I seen it, but I had also listened to it and touched it this way; my perception of flavor came essentially from what my mind offered or took away from me; the only thing it missed must certainly have been revealed by my little book in the secret of its fragments; when the little book lost its power, deprived of its dikes and fortifications, the old Greeks flooded it with their *virgin authority;* then, my lord, like desiccated land suddenly fertile from the rain, it came to be overgrown by buds over which it had no influence; this is how this stimulus was offered to me: through the expression of the tones of my old Parmenides and his counterpart; I read them with no expectations or will to control anything; I welcomed them in this meager freedom, experiencing them, revisiting them over long nights; I breathed in their words, they came to me; I let them roam freely within me, and I within them; no image emerged, no explanation rushed forth, no figurine or theater set invaded the place of our encounters, and the scene evoked by their vibrations was not illuminated; just the articulation of both tones that opened a tiny space; through cross-contamination, when I left my bed and came back to the concert of things surrounding me, despite my anguish, I could simply hear, simply see, simply touch, and simply perceive; I could more importantly not anguish over my mental silence, or regret any of those illusions that flowed from my mind before, overrunning everything, to cover by uncovering, reveal by hiding, and incorporate what I perceived in the mold of an illusion;

FIRST VOICE
. . . the same person, him, he is both thinking and being . . .

I spent entire nights in this strange exchange with strange words; if part of my attention focused on the ground, I was soon able to distract myself from it unwillingly and remain in an intimate conversation with the fragments of the poem; hard to remember, my lord, during which night or moment of these strange readings, for the first time in my life I felt the sensation of simply staring at the *incomprehension,* and even the *unknowable,* with no veil or device, and yet to continue living; each time that at the mouth of the cave I fashioned a hut to shield me from the rain or freezing dews, and that I grabbed this holy little book, the *unknowable* opened before me and deep down inside me, like a landscape without country, a land without borders as empty as a desert but as dense as a tropical forest; when I finally realized it, the verses of the old poet and his counterpart resonated within me in a new way; it was no longer the initial *articulation,* but a *possibility* just as deprived of immediate reality as it was stripped of any tangible limits;

I could only bear it with anguish, endure it like truth without light, which had nowhere to go and which led to no triumph; this possibility offered me only its resonance on my forehead, its expansion in my chest, its emergence in my ears when I moved my lips in a slight whisper; this *possibility* returned to me the feeling of my own existence, as full as everything that lived around me in fearless plentitude;

*

the strangest part, my lord, was that this old poet and his Other appeared to me within the same isolation as me; one told me that the goddess of truth, or truth itself, was kept in the rarely used paths of humankind, in absence and withdrawal, solitude and silence, the impossible kept like a launch pad—and because of this, I felt the island was the outer extremity; the Other then patched together shadow and light, impossible and possible, inhabited the void, intertwined life and death, created incessant movement in what seemed fixed, and instituted a sort of general impulse; as for their arrangement, my lord, it looked like a destroyed temple, of which only a sparkling base would remain, massive and rectilinear yet open to the great sky, and which, in this solidity and openness, allowed every ounce of verticality;

*

I am not well versed in the science of poems, but it seemed to me, my lord, that the old Parmenides had understood that the spectacular unknowable erased all hope, immobilized all possibilities, and thrust life into such anguish that one threw oneself headlong into the emotions, illusions, and chimera, thus forcing all possibilities to swarm all over in what became the maze of life; the Other, his counterpart, then roamed through the maze, and filled it with these complexities and discoveries at each intersection of unsettling perspectives and beautiful horizons; this is where my *point of articulation* was located;

*

in addition, my lord: these two ancient Greek men appeared to be woven more of restraint than effusiveness, more of silence than declamation, and the authority I felt in each of their fragments seemed extremely sober and discreet; as if what they were looking to reveal could never fully be done, never presented in full light, but forever knotted into a secret, into withdrawal, and the uncomfortable views from the shadows; *nature loves to hide;* I had to keep this secret—this anguish—to never stop feeling and experiencing it; to understand that this initial blow immediately conferred upon me energy and renewal toward undertaking this island-maze of which I was now perfectly aware;

*

after a night of reading, I could definitively look at the empty sky without projecting gods and demons onto it; I could look at the ocean without expecting a sail, and without seeing vain hope assault me; and I could look at myself, still under the sympathetic anguish that would capture all my attention; many things that moved me during ordinary times now left me in a continuous state of placidity; goats found strangled in the vines, nestlings devoured by rats; turtle eggs massacred by crabs . . . all this desolation filled me with no particular emotion whatsoever; the only somewhat disturbing feeling that arose were the strange sensations filtered by my lost memory; I heard screams and death rattles, sounds of metal and agony that resonated like echoes; an unknown experience grew within me and filled me with a fog of revolt;

my days became stranger and stranger; I could spend hours observing a seashell's mother-of-pearl; or contemplating for an extended period the quivering of a cabbage leaf; once, I discovered a blue rock under some roots and gazed at it for hours on end, my only activity for a few weeks; I became a bark examiner, a sand watcher; what I saw of birds, insects, and fruits did not surprise me whatsoever, did not cause my mind or soul to budge whatsoever, nor did it have any utility, just to train my eyes to be patient enough to examine their infinite details, which filled

me with tranquility—this anguish that had no end; I even forgot
to drink and eat, and when I did, it was at all hours, and wherever I had stopped roaming, and my food could be anything, a
granadilla that I extended my entire body to reach, the flesh of
palm worms, a sugarcane knot;

I had begun wandering around the island again looking for
nothing in particular; I was happy to go wherever the trade
winds blew me; I could follow a very precise path that the gusts
of air marked into the sharp grass or cut into the crenelated
cliffs; when I stopped, often exhausted, I could pick flowers
and make a flower crown or necklace for no reason, and they
endowed me with different fragrances; otherwise, I took the
time to weave a small hut with specific leaves; making colorful,
fragrant shelters, each time different, and I took refuge in them
like in a palace deprived of pomp; I had built so many fortifications that there almost seemed to be an urgency to developing
these open huts; their sole utility was perhaps to alleviate the
anguish that had become permanent; designing them, looking
at them, and lying in them brought me some relief; often, I did
not even want to sleep or rest there; I was satisfied with my
huts, and I always needed to come back to them, just to refresh
them with flowers and colors, so that they'd remain pretty in
their frivolity;

my eyes had become so sharp that I was able to grow attached
to things that before would have seemed insignificant: a flowering cactus, growing in the crack of a burning rock; shades of
pink quartz in a cove of black sand; small crown-plants hung
to tree trunks that fed by waving their soft, green roots in the
wind; a thousand wildflowers, as tiny as the bugs they attracted
en masse; while contemplating with extreme patience, I wove
something with my now-creative hands; I hung up bizarre
objects everywhere that proclaimed nothing other than their
conceptless shape, their indeliberate movement, their snapshot
perception that proved nothing; the small sound these objects
made as the wind blew never led to song . . . ;

SECOND VOICE
... the prince whose oracle is in Delphi
neither exposes nor hides,
he signals ...

I wandered with an intensity I had never experienced in my whole life; I no longer had a sedentary lifestyle; I felt the frenzy of the trade winds, birds, bees, and rodents, always in flight and in movement; anything motionless must certainly have been plants, but the most rooted plants also engage in incessant movement, with a thousand buds and small sprouts that could be seen radiating around an origin ... ; *and therefore wandering, my lord, I became aware of wandering!* ... ; wandering orients without guidance; it is the mother of freedom; wandering does not lead to discoveries, it is a discovery; it does not show, it is presented to and presents the unpredictable; I had raved a lot during my mental breakdowns, but at present I did not rave; *I had begun to naturally wander;* my body roamed, my mind roamed, nothing oriented me except for my roaming; my whole being followed an imperceptible stream, inscribed in the heart of things; and when I remained motionless in one place, my wandering became still; it prevailed in an inexplicable way that gave me presence of mind in the face of a gigantic *openness* into which, my lord, I had to no other choice than to enter;

*

I understood these great awakenings that seemed motionless, in the most extreme isolation, appearing to be detached from all things and from themselves, and undoubtedly staring down something unthinkable given them to see; they were in fact more active than the wind, more nomadic than all the sailors of England, and better connected right at the heart of things than all the roots of the world could ever be;

*

all of this is really tenuous, my lord, and extremely difficult to pass on, but it is my duty to not give up; I lived an unfettered freedom that densified itself by the day; nothing happened, but an adventure continued beyond my understanding; my mind was not affected, nor the well-being of my mental state; no melancholia tarnished my eye; neither order nor disorder, control nor conquest, indifference nor detachment: *moving* was the only available given; this is what I want to name: a freedom with no compromise that cloistered me no longer, that gave me limitless access to myself and my surroundings; *a coming into relation*;

*

my mental activity, order, morality, reason, sometimes even my moments of disarray, had only helped to protect me from what was there; even this anguish, which had seemingly been a point of departure from my former illusions, was perhaps the very first illusion to compensate for the thunderbolt of *What* which constituted the island; what I thought was my reasoning, what I had spent so many years revering for fear of sinking into animality, was also as much an illusion as the others that reasoning had to compensate for . . . ; it is by imagining that, by repeating it to myself, that I managed to pursue my leisurely contemplations, to create in futility, to wander perpetually; I no longer named things; I no longer strove to recognize anything; I surrendered to my surroundings, in a *relation* that brought me closer while clarifying nothing, that offered a relation to me without ever effacing the irreversible opacity with which I composed it; this opacity was the very ground of what I had experienced and what I would continue to experience on this island: a *What*;

*

this island, my lord—this *What*, this thing—was outside time, eventless, outside the movement of the world, outside any possible future, yet it was in this exact place of distress and suffering

in my soul that the *relation to myself* and to the world must
have been set in motion;

*

I said *What* to help me express this bundle of inexpressible
thoughts; attempting to handle them; I should not have run
away from that harsh reality, but rather face it, keep an eye on
its radiance, cope with the anguish, accept the absence of any
voice, of any path, and, still in its presence, enduring this anguish, to implement everything so as not to neglect it but rather
to develop some life from it;

*

I could not explain how, when, or why I ended up once more
by the footprint; I was not alone; I was both near and far from
every existing thing around me, inside and out, like a fusion
that would accentuate irreducible strangeness; parrots now remained at my side and accompanied my steps; they alighted on
my shoulders or were content to fly from branch to branch a
few feet away; there also was the young goat that now stayed
close by, pretending to ignore me; next to the footprint I had
brought hundreds of wonderful seashells, sumptuous basalts,
dark, polished tree bark, deep blue silicas; small arrangements
of bamboo and fish scales that I spread all around it, so that the
wind made them move and clink together, covering the footprint in sound; inspired by this initial arrangement, I brought
mongoose pelts and small calabashes back from my abandoned
chests, taking the time to tie them together and fashion a set
of wings that could take to the wind, then hung them from an
arch of bamboo; I added a series of very fine sparkling mother-
of-pearl slivers that captured the light as brightly as mirrors
would, and that swirled around endlessly on the end of a string;
once completed, the installation sparked with the morning dew,
caught the low breeze, and spun in the warm wind to attract
butterflies and many dragonflies; shortly after, the beach was
overwhelmed with the most beautiful sounds; the wind and

light, caught by my assembly, had become visible, and accentuated the mystery of the footprint in sound, extremely fluid, often changing, and endless;

it was not a celebration like I once used to have out of madness, it was just to share with the island what I loved; I was thankful for this disruption that had freed me from the idiot; my useless little creations (which I would have much trouble describing, since they came under very pure moments of inspiration) transformed the beach into an unusual place, which jingled, jangled, and jittered in all sorts of ways, and which accompanied this wind as it spun and the sky as it moved; I no longer looked at the footprint trying to understand it, or even to surmise some origin; it was here, inscribed in the mass of clay coated in sand; the footprint was ageless, had neither beginning nor end; it must have certainly been there even before I lived on this planet; perhaps it came from prehistoric times, and its relationship with the shape of my foot only originated in my poor senses; I simply tried to perceive what the footprint was: an inexpressible shape, located here, upon time and the surface of the world, generating its inexpression in the vastest immobility; I could now experience it, feel it, and thereby feed on it;

*

SECOND VOICE
. . . the health of humankind is the reflection of the health of the planet . . .
. . . time is a child at play . . .

*

I tried to breathe imagining myself in this footprint, being a part of it, and it a part of me, with no history, except to be in *relation* with it; this footprint did not open to any Other but me; in no way did it open onto just anyone, nor even to some kind of imaginative *presence*; I do not really know how to say it, my lord, and I know how confusing all of this is, but it can only remain as such; the old Greeks had taught me: *the relevance of what is said holds in what is not said, in what it shows and whose sign it carries;* these useless creations that I had organized around the footprint were just as much signs toward the unknowable, the uncertain, the unthinkable, in which movements, sounds, and a disused radiance were found; it had made *an artist* of me; inclined toward the footprint that now seemed to me like the opening of an infinite beginning; my lord, the footprint opened to the spectacular and remained here, completely affixed to my mind, with which I had to, without telling myself stories, experience infinite possibilities and maintain an open relationship;

*

it is difficult to tell you if this was the place of my final birth; anyway, I kept this mind-set for as long as possible; I felt no motivation whatsoever to build, hunt, or control this place, only the huge desire to perceive this *What* that the natural splendor of the island allowed me to imagine, and that was within the island, just as it was within me; I believed for a long time that it came down to life itself, to the awareness of living or being alive, but even the extension of this consciousness and the great passionate inspirations that it provided me with seemed artificial to me; I then returned to a keen perception of this thing that was impossible to define, that in the past fed all powers, that filled all the *presences* with life, and that now forced my mind to remain on the uncomfortable path of a thousand possibilities in the making; since then, all seemed not empty, absent, or fearless, but open, an *openness* that opened to the most fecund despair, to the most serene anguish, to the most lucid joy, to the least harmful illusion, to the alliances of shadow and light, from the unthinkable and from everything that could be thought; it must have been the happiest moment of my life, a happiness where I went without God, without the devil, without some belief to send my mind into an old maze; nothing other than the sudden appearance of anguish, the intense passing of nausea, the pomp of a fine malaise from time to time, but they no longer provoked any panic whatsoever in me, just the sensation of an immense beginning: an inaugural place where I could finally build in a consciousness that was bare, very rough, as extremely solitary as it was supportive, everything I could be;

*

SECOND VOICE
... invisible harmony is worth much more than the one
that is visible ...

at the end of all of this, my lord, I had fallen *into awareness,* or rather into this anguished questioning about what I was on this island, hanging on to this question like an unreachable sun just like a *mapian,* as plantation negroes say about these wounds that never heal ... ;

*

just to say, my lord, that I was barely moved to see the huge sail of your ship appear from the tip of the headland; I would go there every morning to open up, my mind and body carried by the wind; butterflies escorted me, but also wood pigeons and a couple of moorhen, magnetized by my presence; parrots followed the same ritual as well as a few other goats that had met with my hard-headed goat; there was a tortoise always to my left, paced perfectly in time with my easy stride; from atop this sharp, rocky cliff, covered in thousands of little crabs, I discovered the sails of your brig that peacefully progressed, at a safe distance from the barrier of the cays; I thus knew that you were already acquainted with this place; it should have been a magical show for my poor mind; how it had long desired to see a sail! ... had long called for it in my many mad moments and feverish illusions! ... ; but now, I just tried to discover the ship in these rays of light that brought life to every source of power that will come to be;

I recognized the maneuver easily, you had to look for a cove in order to set a few rowing boats afloat; I was extremely visible from the headland; the brilliant sparkles that caught the sun like little lightning bolts must certainly have been your spyglasses pointed toward me, examining me; I peacefully continued my ceremony of the winds, then I returned to my little cave where I made sure to don a few nice necklaces, very fine animal pelts, to braid the hair that fell to my shoulders and perfume it with cinnamon; I also grabbed the parasol of foliage that I picked each week from a tree whose leaves were the perfect shape, and I headed toward the beach where your rowboats would certainly berth;

I was neither moved, nor frightened, nor impatient to face these men; I was only carried by a plentitude neither blissful, nor worried, but certain, all spherical and powerful, with no quaking, and that now my lord, a surge of beauty accompanied me; after twenty-five years of this motionless adventure, I have now come full circle with this immense encounter . . .

Captain's Log

September 26—In the year of our Lord 1659—We saw him. My intuition had not misled me. It occurred at the first hour of the morning, the ship sailed alongside the shore toward the cove on which I had landed twelve years ago. Returning was an adventure that I enjoyed leading. I had in this way sowed many islands with chickens, pigs, and at times even rats inadvertently, and it was always a surprise to find whole packs on other journeys, as if these little islands had the ability to multiply the slightest bit of life that was entrusted to them. It allowed us to lightly sow these deserted lands with meat. We, of the Old World, transformed these islands into wild gardens and natural farming lands. But now, it was unusual, and my heart beat differently. What I was searching for, in the eyepiece of my spyglass, was a man. I eventually saw him.

It was the officer of the deck that found him from the maintop, and who called on me to confirm what he thought he had seen. He was right. It was him. Still alive. I was surprised by his stature. His head was covered in long braids like a pharaoh. His beard was also braided beautifully and hung to his chest. He was dressed in animal pelts, nicely brushed, cut, and sewn in the tradition of his people and land. His skin was very tanned and hugged his fine, thin muscles of iron. The features that I examined with my spyglass confirmed that it was him. It made me more emotional than I would have thought.

I ordered the approach maneuvers and mooring arrangements to be accelerated in front of the small cove. Then, I dispatched rowboats to meet him. The men who went were armed, because quite often when we find survivors on a desert island like this, they have lost their minds and become dangerous. They landed ashore in military docking procedure, covered by two twelve-pounder long guns and a bombard.

But the castaway appeared in front of our men with majestic slowness and profound tranquility, as if we were opposite a wise man from around the Nile River in the time of the pyramids, where the Greeks were said to have studied. I rejoined the docking crew without delay, curious to see how he would react upon seeing me again. He did not recognize me. He did not recognize anything. He was just happy to see us, to see human beings, and all these years did not seem to have overly affected him. He just said that he had lived here for some twenty-five years, which was an acceptable mistake, as in these types of isolation, time often plays tricks on us. He had only been there for twelve years. The strange thing was that he offered bouquets of flowers and tawdry knickknacks he had fashioned and of which he seemed to make a stately ceremony.

I had him brought aboard, and I received him in my cabin, accompanied by the surgeon to whom I had already explained the matter. We welcomed him with a bit of Spanish wine, dry biscuits, a few slices of fresh meat, and a red bean stew accompanied by cod. I had the table set with cutlery, silverware, and a beautiful chandelier. He had not forgotten any of his table manners, but he spoke with a loud voice like those that the solitude had sapped for far too long. He called me "lord," not owing to my rank, but most certainly because of what I represented for him from the world he had lost. My face, my voice did not arouse any emotion. I realized that he had completely lost his memory. Still recognizable, he was however no longer the one that I had abandoned on these shores twelve years ago.

I was astonished by the narrative of his journey on the island. An endless mental torment, close to delirium, a motionless adventure, tortuous like the maze he had wandered. He said he was able to overcome it, which made him into the man who was before us: a knowledgeable man. *I am,* he repeated, *a knowledgeable man.* He talked without catching his breath, in a series of sentences and events, progressing in spirals, as one could hear in the traditional rhetoric of griots in villages of Negritia. He was not telling stories, by the way; he said, or tried, rather, before us, with us, to offer a "snapshot" of what he had experienced and what he had become.

Astounded, I looked at him with compassion. There was no longer any trace of that young Dogon sailor, educated from the Quran and Egyptian texts and skilled at almost everything, that I had picked up in my early trading years on the African shores. He had completed a few voyages with me between the Old and New Worlds. At the time, his name was Ogomtemmêli, the son of a line of great knowledgeable hunters, but I never ascertained whether this was his real name. He had become a true sailor, with great expertise in everything, from navigating to using his long hands. I had taught him everything I knew, and he had passed on just as much to me. Up until the day the cable cracked his skull, and if he survived, the damage sustained was so great that he forgot who he was and what he was doing on the ship. The most irritating part was that his behavior had become strange, pure madness, with eccentricities

that plunged the crew into fear and risked attract-
ing the evil eye on us. Out of desperation, not knowing where to put him, I had him chained with our
merchandise at the time, which relieved us but certainly resulted in him losing his mind. He could not
stand all those captives stocked in the hold, and
these corpses that each morning we threw into the
water as we continued to navigate toward the new
continent. We had however practiced this business
together once or twice along the shores of Guinea
without troubling him too much. But his madness
intensified in the hold and led him to further outrage
and violence, which was unacceptable for maintaining safety onboard. With dissatisfaction spreading
throughout the crew, I decided to abandon him on
some desert island, like we used to do for captives
who were rabid, contagious, or possessed by an evil
spirit.

So that it take place without incident, I ordered
him knocked unconscious at dawn. We had maneu-
vered around the island that we must have looked
for while taking great risks, in a land infested with
cays for shipwrecks. A rowboat transported him and
threw him on the sand of this little cove where a
frigate lay, seemingly having wrecked there in very
old times. I had a lump in my throat, but I hoped he
would survive. He had the capacity and the courage
to do so. I had known many negroes, sailors or captives, abandoned like this for a thousand reasons,
who went on to mix with the savages until they had
become true black cannibals. To help him, I had my
shoulder harness tied to his waist with my name engraved on it, a beautiful saber, and some food in a
barrel. I was touched to hear the use he had made
of the name.

The rowboat was unfortunately unable to berth. We had not chosen the right angle. The sailors decided to throw him overboard a few cable lengths away from the beach, tied down to a barrel, making sure that the current took him to the shore. This indeed happened, as we observed with the spyglass while pulling away from these much too dangerous cays. We then resumed our voyage toward Brazil where my plantation expected me, and with time I had forgotten this son, this good friend, this brother.

All the years had passed by without much thought. This voyage close by had reminded me of the memory and affection that I felt for our castaway. We listened to him all night long, not completely understanding what he meant by his multiple births in his solitude in this lonely place. He was aware that he had undergone a fine transformative adventure. He was no longer the kind man I had once known, but a man full of serenity and joyful seriousness, able to laugh, and whose very eyes could draw you in, could pass through you and immediately expose you. I did not have the courage to remind him of what he had been, nor especially of the sad incident that had tragically separated us. This is why I hid my name from him. To conclude, he showed us the little book that had helped him so much, a small, black, crumpled book, covered with half-erased fragments. Some had been copied from an almost illegible, tormented, at times even senseless writing. The surgeon, who fancied literature, believed to have recognized two of the old philosophers of ancient Greece, Parmenides and presumably Heraclitus, and was amazed that such obscure texts could have encouraged survival efforts. To which the knowledgeable man mysteriously responded that at the heart of the most obscure part lies a light, that shadow and light form one whole sphere.

The next morning, I begged him to stay with us, which he refused, in the same way he refused everything else we gave him. He declared in his mixing of several languages and strange accent that the island was his home, and that in this place, he was at the heart of himself and of the world, and in all the places of the world at once. Which I identified as a form of delirium. Things turned bad when the screams began to rise up from the ship's hold. The captives started to experience one of their collective crises, which were always unpredictable. The memories must have flooded back to him then. Fire blazed in his eyes. He looked at us strangely and pinched our skin while looking at his own, which was of course sunburned and thus of a darker pigmentation, which he seemingly realized. This put him in a state of extremely confused emotions. He started speaking in his ancient language, perhaps without even understanding what he said. He stormed out of the cabin, rushed to the deck yelling, and demanded the hold to be opened. He wanted to free the captives and bring them with him to the island.

The men could not control him. He was of uncommon strength, and showed such determination in the confrontation that alas we were forced to shoot him from afar. I was very sad because of this misfortune. I ordered that he receive honors and be given the prayer for the dead in a shroud from our ship. Then, I took the time to have him buried in a gully, not too far from the shore. Curious about what he had told me, I performed a little tour of the island accompanied by my surgeon to look for a few of the things he had confided to us. The island seemed intact, neither fields, nor pipes nor mills, nor the first storehouse or repurposed cave. I did not find any trace whatsoever of human life that would have subsisted here over all these years. It was only an island of forgotten times and fixed eternities. As for the footprint, we could not find it anywhere.

*

In the year of our Lord 1659.
I do not remember the exact date.
I picked up my logbook again after all these weeks.

We departed this island not knowing that the weather would turn, that the sea would move, or that the ocean would drift us toward a shipwreck from which I would be the only survivor. I did not know that I would now have to undergo what my unfortunate victim had just experienced before me, as if by prophecy, using my name.

Now in his situation, alone, and lost on a similar island, these first words that I am writing in my poor logbook are for him, to ask for forgiveness, but also to position my survival in line with his strange experience. I prayed to the Heavens for it to strengthen me, and for it to help me survive . . . but that is a whole other story . . .

*

"September 30, 1659.—I, poor miserable Robinson Crusoe, being shipwrecked during a dreadful storm in the offing, came ashore on this dismal, unfortunate island, which I called *The Island of Despair;* all the rest of the ship's company having drowned, and myself almost dead."

This journal was recovered in the chests of the ship-wrecked captain, merchant of Guinea, who was rescued more than thirty years later, and who would

*tell of his incredible adventure on this forgotten is-
land in the Americas.*

Favorite, March 2008–July 2010.

THE FOOTPRINT WORKSHOP
Leftover Lines and Notes

Rereading Daniel Defoe's magnificent opus (1719). It had remained open like a light in my memory. Childhood sustenance. Dreams. I was really taken by it, like millions of children across the world. I had imagined myself a thousand times on the desert island. And sooner or later, I knew I would do something with it.

*

Defoe exerts innocent narrative energy, he tells a story, and it works. I envy his innocence of another century. One can read it, but one can no longer write it.

*

Defoe's Crusoe is civilized and civilizes.
Michel Tournier's Crusoe is humanized and humanizes.
One can only continue the humanization process. To look deeper there.

*

The "Crusoe adventure" is an archetype of individuation; this is why the story continues to fascinate us, it is ever inexhaustible.

*

Defoe's fiction searches for the truth effect. The details. The narrative. The verisimilitude. Reality assists the story in a silent contrast. One believes in it, that's what it's meant for. But beyond the verisimilitude, and in spite of it, Defoe creates an excessiveness, and this is where his novel radiates. It is perhaps the main reality of the novel, regardless of time period: *its excessiveness—what reality cannot accept.*

*

Tournier's Crusoe is admirable and impressive. He explores the precious "Crusoe adventure" in depth, leaving no stone unturned. His fiction is already distant, he tears it apart, and draws the narrative away to look deeper into each moment, questioning time and space, interrogating the silences, the untold stuff of human existence, A beautiful sphere of excess to which one feels as though he has nothing to add to it at first. Perhaps just flickers of dizziness, cracks, and distortions . . .

*

I will have spent my whole life writing intuitions from my childhood. Sometimes, one needs an entire lifetime to understand one's childhood.

*

Writing explores, one must allow it to delve deeper, to leave things to chance, and to yearn for what it unexpectedly brings back. One needs to celebrate writing when it brings back the unexpected, to train writing for the unexpected, for the freedom of making discoveries—that are even more wonderful when they reach, incredibly, into the very heart of seeming trivialities.

*

Finding great expanses in trivialities and inertia, the minor and immobile ones. Going toward what only writing knows of reality and of the human condition. This is when the story explodes in the "snapshot" that Glissant talks about.

*

It's funny, I inject subtle distortions into the situation, take pleasure in seeing them work like waves of imperceptible transformation. The unreal must be lightweight, the fantastic must feel like a breath. In this context, too much of the unreal would paradoxically only bring back reality. I like this idea of gaps very much . . .

*

The semicolon became necessary, I do not know why, maybe the idea of stream of consciousness, of mental instability, of typing a story that tells no tales. It is not Flaubert's semicolon.

*

As an existential situation, Crusoe's is precious. Through the individuation process, it consists of the beginning, the origin, or rather a return to the origin when reality has exhausted all horizons and resources. It is precious for us today, in these rushes of the world into its totalities.

*

The individual has always haunted groups, hordes, tribes, nations, and civilizations. The wonders and insanities of the individual will create the necessity for the group. All these communities kept the unpredictable and threatening individuation process on a tight leash. All human development increases the individual equation. All heroes (or villains) are individuals who shake up and fascinate communities. Defoe's Crusoe fascinated us because he could reconfigure everything from his position— the secret dream of everyone . . . The challenge of today.

*

Stepping between Defoe and Tournier, between two masses of light. To find the gap.

*

The semicolon is an energy smuggler. I am now discovering it. Like a real cool bootlegger that belles lettres have mistakenly seen as a small telegraph operator. Error.

*

Life teaches us the following: there is no existence without constantly experimenting with infinite possibilities. The radiance of a *presence* (a flash of life) comes as much from possibilities realized as from possibilities triggered by this very radiance, and being part of this flash, without so much as being activated.

*

If I am incapable of changing while exchanging, I become petrified, therefore I alter myself. Without the idea of Relation, we lose what is alive. In Heraclitus's river, the bather changes as much as the water in which he bathes, hence the radical impossibility of two identical baths.

*

"... *in my discourses among them, I had frequently given them an account of my two voyages to the coast of Guinea: the manner of trading with the negroes there, and how easy it was to purchase upon the coast for trifles—such as beads, toys, knives, scissors, hatchets, bits of glass, and the like—not only gold-dust, Guinea grains, elephants' teeth, &c., but negroes, for the service of the Brazils, in great numbers.*" It's sad: Defoe's Crusoe was a slave trader.

*

Here, the adventure was internal and mental, almost motion-less. The story ferments, glimpsing states of perception. The hard part is allowing the small bubbles to burst, which create events, like light.

*

Gathering together Defoe's old-fashioned expressions and old clichéd phrases lends the text a quaint feel that really pleases me, like a bit of old flesh. But I also like the distortion that makes my Crusoe think and speak like today. The island is in a time warp. What matters is the existential situation in relation to our contemporary challenges, all the rest has already been exhausted, and beautifully so.

*

I like taking another look at Defoe's and Tournier's twists and turns, rewriting them in my own way. Like a palimpsest, the initial image is all the way at the bottom, powerful and beau-tiful, and the more I work on it, the more it washes off, and something else rises to the top, as an extension, possibly un-earthed . . . the background music remains.

*

Here, the "I" is a herd.

*

To no longer tell stories, to trigger possibilities. To explode the twists and turns into bubbles of perception.

*

To give up the narrative and to sow possibilities, endlessly.

*

His Highness's book, *Contre la philosophie,** comes along at just the right time and continually nourishes me. He projects us toward the original impossibility. He sends us back to the founding impotence. He throws us into panic like this. For me, he reinforces the trajectory of my Crusoe.

*

We return to the beginning of thought, but also to the beginning of art. The origin is modern, and much more: it is ahead of us, as Edgar Morin, like Heidegger, reminds us. And it's true that all life, all art, is worth something only in its relation to the initial unthinkable. The first burst of awareness was afflicted by the unknowns of human life and the terrifying absurdity of death. This is what is at work beneath each attempt to put reality, magic, and religions in order, to think about or aestheticize it. This is the fundamental adventure. This is the footprint.

*

His Highness turns the philosopher into an artist. He is right. The artist is at the beginning, and also at the end.

*

Being as an "impotent" power. A shame, such a negative connotation for so much plenitude. I tried out the notion of "fearlessness" but it wasn't much better. Parmenides's *"there is"* is still the best: an undefined neutrality.

*

"The eternal silence of these infinite spaces terrifies me." Blaise Pascal. Some fine honey for this footprint.

*

---

* Guillaume Pigeard de Gurbert, *Contre la philosophie* (Actes Sud, 2010).

Weigh the unthinkable. This is the point of departure for all belief, thought, art, writing, as for an interminable quake, and endless exploration. It is also the impact from which the awareness begins its migration toward the center of the mind . . .

*

My Highness sends me this precious reminder about Pascal: "*When I see the blindness and the misfortune of man, when I regard the silent universe, and man without light, left to himself, and, as it were, lost in this corner of the universe, unaware of who has put him there, what he has come to do, what will become of him at death, and incapable of knowing everything, I become terrified, like a man who was allegedly carried in his sleep to a dreadful desert island, and would awake without knowing where he is, and with no means of escape. And thereupon I wonder how people in so wretched a state do not fall into despair. I see other people around me of a like nature. I ask them if they are better informed than I. They tell me that they are not. And thereupon these wretched strays, having looked around them, and seen some pleasing objects, have given in and become attached to them. For my own part, I have been unable to attach myself to them, and, considering how strongly it appears that there is something else beyond what I see, I have examined whether this God would have left some sign of Himself.*" Pascal, *Pensées*, no. 693, ed. Léon Brunschvicg. Some good logwood honey. Pascal is a human being.

*

My Crusoe brings me back to Derek Walcott and Saint-John Perse. It's always surprising how writing calls out other writings, awakens books, fills libraries with life. Writing can be found within layers already present, already explored, that this new conscience brings into bright light, a new beginning that is filled with wonder. *Sentimenthèque! Feelibrary!* A sentimental library. Actually, any advancement of awareness brings us back to the splendor of the origin, it's guaranteed . . .

*

As each conscience reaches maturity, *sentimenthèques* help us get started.

*

The place of the future is intact in the origin.

*

There are always way too many words. One must spend hours and days reading and rereading to find the word in excess. Each word cut deserves a trophy; sometimes, the sentence becomes too dry and they come back in force and are happy to do so . . . Musicality has the final say.

*

Strange how the semicolon doesn't stop rather it rushes. Sometimes, it delays slightly, but nevertheless speeds up. Soap.

*

Variation on Crusoe—I like this idea. Any creation is in some way a variation. The same work projected onto the horizon, the old foundation of a temple, which gives way to cathedrals . . .

*

I like this impossibility: a fixed adventure, motionless, something to drive Defoe or Stevenson to despair. It isn't a renunciation of the story, the narrative. It's a renunciation of the naive narrative, one that would be believable, that would be taken seriously, and that would consider fiction as reality. What matters is the situation to endlessly explore, in its ineffable, unthinkable, impossible ways . . . The narrative yields before the "telling" that *captures*, surprises and is surprised, decomposes parts of reality, goes on forever, examines the details, explodes the insignificant, searches, immobilizes, renounces itself, thereby renewing itself . . .

*

. . . in fact over these twenty years I had held on to my humanity, but simply locked within my illusions and body, fortress of flesh and mental island on this prison-like island;—Leftover line.

*

A beautiful modernity in the Crusoe situation: the fact that he is forced to reconstruct himself on a purely individual basis. This had to supply the fantasies of all the individualities restrained in the community corsets of cultures and civilizations. It already reflected the contemporary individuation and its problems. The question is how to grow without the crutch of communities and their standards of civilization.

*

Actually, it is the individual satisfaction that opens onto the widest and newest solidarities. Individual satisfaction opens to the idea of *Relation*. Selfishness, nonsolidarity, every person for themselves, is in reality a sickness of individuation exacerbated by capitalism.

*

From time to time, I engage with the details as Defoe does. I just add useless and insignificant detail to extend them as far as possible. One can feel that the details begin to quake like a new horizon right away.

*

The absence of others causes damage at various levels of consciousness, reducing or transforming them into an infinite amount of illusions. One side of consciousness structures itself with others, or the absence thereof. The Other, however, is like a cyclone that suddenly appears, a panic that shakes the beautiful structures formed with others or the idea we conceive of it. The Other, in its extreme, is the unthinkable one.

*

The question of others is less decisive for us than that of the Other.

*

My Crusoe does not have a Bible, but Parmenides's Poem, and fragments of Heraclitus. I had always thought that I, too, would have brought a Bible with me onto the desert island, but the idea of a Parmenidean poem, obscure little sun that drops us in front of a fearless *being;* and of the other, my dear Heraclitus, who keeps complexifying reality, matching opposites, linking antagonisms in a unity of fire, and who dispatches everything to an incessant future, seems to maintain a limitless place capable of feeding a hundred years of solitude.

*

Parmenides, Heraclitus, Perse, Glissant, Césaire, Walcott, Faulkner . . . all shaded and obscure. Transparency only opens to the idea of a fully illuminated truth . . . quickly nullified by the mysterious crushing reality.

*

Heraclitus would have liked that: the immense solitude that opens onto a horizontal Relation with a whole island, continent, and planet. This withdrawal of humans that opens onto all people and onto the necessity of the most wonderful relationship possible with them. The connection lies in solitude. Solitude is the highest level of proximity.

*

The worst part about loneliness is when it does not open to any solitude.

*

... *all that my excitement, my alleged discoveries, my various thoughts and sensations, had done was to cover this "thing" that now stood in front of me, and that I perceived with some horror deep within me* ... —Leftover line.

*

There is no reality, only imaginary. This is why art is precious: it creates reality and feeds imaginaries, taking them out of their petrification that is seen as reality.

*

This beautiful citation of Nietzsche, that I find in Jean Beaufret's *Parmenides*: "*I traced the origins. Then, I became foreign to all its reverence. Everything became strange around me, everything became solitude. But even this, deep inside, that which can revere, rose up in secret. Then the shadow of the tree I sat under began to grow, the tree of becoming* ..."—I am happy with that. All of it resonates here ...

*

... *what I had before me was a continuous proliferation that took all the essence, all the appearances in the imperative of becoming* ... —Leftover line.

*

Telling it all means to point out the untold instead of trying to deny it.

*

Each narration must come about in the inenarrable's presence.

*

. . . the world I had deployed on the island came from the ship; I had thought that through it I would find that civilization again buried somewhere deep within; but here, among these common water hyacinths, in the radiant wonder that transformed all these backwater insects, with a placidity identical to that of the big yellow toads that surrounded me, I understood that deep within me, there wasn't more humanity than civilization, only an innocent aptitude to connect, exchange, share with every living thing, and to grow as best as possible with it . . .—Leftover line.

*

. . . from time to time, I went to visit my old properties, pasturelands, grazing lands, fortifications, administrative offices, departments of weights and customs; they were all abandoned and invaded; but each time I was on site, I felt like a singular vitality, different from the one that I perceived in the other untouched parts of the island; through observation, I realized that my impact had provoked a particular blossoming, occasionally after tossing fruit seeds. Anyway, it was a minor change that had modified the traditional plant world and favored the new blooms, which had attracted such-and-such insect, such-and-such animal unknown to this area; somehow wherever I had stayed, cockroaches would abound, or ants, or earthworms, and certain birds that had all incorporated my impact into the elements of their survival; each time, I had caused ruptures, small mixtures, and tiny mutations that, on the whole island, went on indefinitely . . .—Leftover line.

*

... I had to go and come back from the dead many times, and the only memory I kept was a translucent melancholia that immerses a landscape in poetry and fire, and that sometimes intensifies here and there, like public streetlights in a desert ...—Leftover line.

*

Only in the explosion of consciousness can one significantly express that which is impossible to say.

*

Each thought must name the unthinkable and be disseminated with it.

*

Renouncing all certitudes absent from uncertainty in a fertile and faithful way.

*

One must always seize the inextricable and enshroud simplicity in ambiguous complexity.

*

The most beautiful impulse comes from impossibility. We should spend time with this beauty—or rather let it surprise us.

*

... yet in this impervious thing, I detected the scent and beauty of flowers, the shock of moon nights. I still tasted the succulence of fruits. My senses arranged the world as necessary to make it

intelligible to me, and to allow me to experience it; the differ-ence was tiny but nevertheless considerable; I was now capable of distancing them and watching them grow . . .—Leftover line.

*

World-literature, it's nonsense . . . the world is certainly today an extremely fine and fair object of literature, as Glissant says, but no one can categorically state what literature will make of it. Beauty may still emerge in what is small, national, rooted in a language, individual, nonglobal . . . we must wait for the major shock, which will signify what is outdated and provide us with a new measure of the horizon, or rather a disproportion-ate one . . .

*

As for thoughts, like for any creation, the impossibility of know-ing and doing is found at the beginning and the end.

*

. . . there was no other world, nor any other reality, than this thing, this bright, unbearable, dauntless light, this unknowable world practically motionless that is; and on the other hand, what our mind, our senses, our creations will make of this world without losing the original malaise, and without any il-lusion about their meager spreading . . .—Leftover line.

*

It is through the relationship with the unthinkable and the impossible that each thought finds its most profound vibra-tion and pertinence. The same goes for each creation and each expression.

*

At the heart of any meaning, there is senselessness. It also constitutes the perspective and the horizon.

*

It is in the initial, irreversible shadow that one optimally creates the glimmer that is our own.

*

The most beautiful Word does nothing but point out the original silence that troubles it.

*

What Parmenides calls *being* is perhaps what Heraclitus named *nature*.

*

What matters is not how the novel progresses, rather finding new ways to tell a story. The novel may be European, but telling a story is undeniably human.

*

... *all of my torment was but a derivation of the primordial torment; the original fire that the old poet had stared at without even trembling* . . .—Leftover line.

*

The unthinkable is the original or generative strike of thought. The impossible is the original or generative strike of all possibilities.
The uncertain is the original or generative strike of the slightest certainty.

*

The prettiest, the truest part of recollection is when it foresees a future.

*

. . . I had to be continuously reborn according to the magnitude of the original shock.
Therein lies all greatness as well as greatest danger . . .—Leftover line.

*

Idiotic fiction is exposed when it vacates the realm of the untellable or ineffable. The allure of a snapshot narrative is its blazing inscription within a generative anguish, like Joyce, Faulkner, Perse, Glissant, Césaire, or García Márquez.

*

I am now discovering the last word of my Crusoe: *encounter.* Any full individuation leads to this foundational space. The encounter.

AFTERWORD
Patrick Chamoiseau's Ecological Footprint

Valérie Loichot

When you step into Patrick Chamoiseau's *Crusoe's Footprint,*
don't expect action but welcome meditation. Chamoiseau's
amorous prose mirrors his noninvasive stance toward the island, the land, and the planet. Jeffrey Landon Allen and Charly
Verstraet's fluid and sensitive translation opens a window for
English-speaking readers onto what is arguably the more concrete literary illustration of the Martinican writer's ecological
thought, which aims for a zero ecological footprint.[1] Like the
French writer Michel Tournier, who had already inverted the hierarchies between Crusoe and Friday featured in Daniel Defoe's
1719 matrix text, Chamoiseau makes Crusoe an African man,
his identity as Dogon revealed in the last pages of the narrative.[2]
The stranded man is above all human, but making him African allows Chamoiseau to highlight the slave trade's entanglement with European hunger to dominate the planet. In this, the
Anthropocene, or the epoch-scale negative impact of humans
on Planet Earth, is undeniably connected to the enslavement
of humans.[3] In his "Leftover Lines and Notes" affixed to the
text, Chamoiseau laments: "It's sad: Defoe's Crusoe was a slave
trader" (162).

To further radicalize Tournier's gesture, Chamoiseau intro-
duces another omnipresent character in the novel, whose voice
is constant and loud: the landscape and its components of shells,
rocks, winds, sand, waves, turtles, pearls, and crabs. In his call
for our mindful listening to the mineral, vegetal, elemental, and
animal beings that compose the island-world, Chamoiseau de-
centers Crusoe, who is there, with no human companion, yet
not alone. The main character of the novel is the island itself.
A silent presence that was not central in earlier Robinsonades,

and was domesticated, conquered, used, and abused by the co-
lonial, now reasserts itself and lives on regardless, of the small
human adventure. The plot of the text, "twenty-five years of
[a] motionless adventure" (150), which lacks sharp actions or
events, constitutes another illustration of the necessary humility
of human agency for nature as we know it to go on.

With this in mind, we can read the presence of the stranded
human on the island as a microcosmic illustration of the journey of humanity on the planet. Indeed, the small island espouses
world-like dimensions: "disparities in the landscape which came
simultaneously from the North and South, East and West; I was
surprised by this incredible variety of microclimates in such a
tiny space" (39). The book is divided into three sections, inter-
rupted by four excerpts from the "Captain's Log," strategically
placed at the very beginning, in two middle sections, and in the
end of the narrative. The voice of the slave trader captain thus
controls the plot, in an attempt to tame time into a human cage
with beginning, middle, and end. This is in sharp contrast with
Crusoe's evolving sense of time, who has relinquished its drive
to control the earth with a single plot of narrative.

The normative use of capital letters in the "Captain's Log"
sections asserts this human control. In contrast, the main body
of the text, told by the stranded human, almost completely
avoids capital letters, as if the voice of the human was itself
unmarked, in a humble fluidity with the voices of the island.
Entour, the French version of the Creole *antou*, a word defining a surrounding where the "human" and "natural" binary
collapses, is more appropriate than "nature" or "landscape" to
define Chamoiseau's earth-model where human gestures are
but one manifestation of agency among the many gestures and
voices of the mineral, the animal, the vegetal, and the monumental elemental of earth and sea. Toward the end of his narrative, the stranded human understands that he has attained
"a freedom with no compromise that cloistered me no longer,
that gave me limitless access to myself and my surroundings"
("à moi-même et à l'entour," *Empreinte*, 214). Understandably,
the translators chose to render the obscure French Creole noun
entour as the term "surroundings" to gain more fluidity. In this

epilogue, however, I maintain the word *entour*, since it does justice to Chamoiseau's ecological thinking whereby, ideally, the human-made and the natural collapse as discrete categories. The word *entour* also indicates the presence of the influential thought of Édouard Glissant, Chamoiseau's teacher, friend, and cowriter.[4] Not only does the word *entour* refer to a Caribbean relationship to the earth, but it also espouses Glissant's philosophy of Relation, in which hierarchies fall and narratives multiply. The stranded human is aware of this when he refers to his being-in-the-world-among-many-others as a "coming into relation" (145).[5]

Yet, there is a plot. The stranded man's twenty-five years spent with no other human company, ghost, or reflection other than the titular footprint, which stubbornly appears, disappears, and reappears, are organized in three sections. These correspond to the three stages of the man on the island, which, I argue, provide a miniature of the presence of humanity on earth: "The Idiot," "The Small Person," and "The Artist." These moments represent (1) conquest (Humanity Is an Idiot), (2) the realization that humans are powerless in the face of the monumental strength of the planet (Humanity Is a Small Person), and (3) the wishful stage where humans enact beauty onto the *entour* and worship it (Humanity Is an Artist). The captain's log, which steals the last word, shatters this last vision by reasserting the idiocy of conquest and domination of the land, personified in the murder of our humble hero.

The Idiot: Colonizing Hubris

The first section of the book, entitled "The Idiot," pictures the first twenty years of the stranded man on the forsaken island. After a brief rebirth in deprivation of material and memory possessions ("I was born once again into the year I knew nothing of . . ." [9]), the man soon re-creates on the island the human history of conquest and exploitation in a gesture he calls "un recommencement de civilisation" (*Empreinte*, 23; "rebuild civilization" [12]). He pillages the schooner: "a frigate I had explored and plundered like an Oriental cave, like a chronicle of the Western world, a relic of all humanity" (11); asserts his sole human authority under a single God: "what mattered was being Robinson Crusoe, only master after God, and lord of this island" (14); and assumes, in one sentence, economic, political, and epistemological power and control: "I must have been . . . an engineer of a certain science, a structural engineer, or plantation master, or naval captain" (43). At this stage, the Western world expresses itself through pillage, monotheism, science, and plantation economy. A similar madness for progress led the poet Paul Valéry to make his famous pronouncement, in his 1919 *La crise de l'esprit*, "We later Civilizations . . . we too now know that we are mortal." Valéry's comment on the nations devastated by the Great War as sunken ships ("empires sunk without a trace, gone down with all their men and all their machines," "the phantoms of great ships") are reminiscent of Chamoiseau's shipwreck as a result of conquest.[6]

During the conquest phase, the island is a void monstrosity: "turning my back to an island that I cared nothing for, this place seemed . . . deserted yet teeming" (15). Skipping the stages of sustainable agriculture, Crusoe reproduces cash-crop plantation practices such as tobacco and coffee cultures, which, on a planetary scale, weigh heavily on an ecological footprint. This stage coincides with the appearance of an indelible human footprint near the beach ("it was a human footprint" [26]). Following our reading of the island as world and of the man as humanity, the human footprint comes to represent the ecological footprint. "Crusoe's footprint" is also humanity's ecological footprint on the planet, which accounts for the pressure put by humans on "natural" resources.

The taming, conquest, and exploitation of the island is enmeshed with Western civilization. Our protagonist explains: "I started to inhabit my name, *Robinson Crusoe* . . . the objects brought back from the frigate nourished my imagination with a western perspective: I was a prince, Castilian, knight . . ." (18). The proclamation "J'habiterai mon nom" (I will live in my name) is a direct homage to Guadeloupe-born poet and Nobel Prize winner Saint-John Perse, who derived, also from Defoe's text, a series of nine poems entitled *Images à Crusoé* (Images for Crusoe). Perse's poem is already inscribed in Chamoiseau's original French title, *L'empreinte à Crusoé*, which mimics the grammar and the gesture of offering in Perse's title. *Images à Crusoé* was written in 1904 by seventeen-year-old Saint-John Perse, a white man born into a family of lawyers and planters in Guadeloupe, a self-described "exile" in the French city of Pau. In the poems, an old man, Crusoé, is stranded not on a deserted island but in a frigid, wall-locked, and nauseating French town (see, for instance, the poem "Le Mur," *Oeuvres complètes*, Pléiade, 12). Perse's Crusoe's lost world is the island, paralleling Perse's exile from his native Guadeloupe, amid his family's bankruptcy. Locked away from his island retrievable only in poetry and nostalgia, Perse's poetic voice elects his name as home and island: "J'habiterai mon nom" ("Exil," ibid., 135).

Chamoiseau invites this foray into Perse through his title, his borrowings, and his direct reference to the poet in the "Footprint Workshop" placed at the end of the book: "My Crusoe brings me back to Derek Walcott and Saint-John Perse" (165). This homage to Perse is a tortured one, since Chamoiseau not only embraces the poet's fellow Caribbeanness but also acknowledges his problematic nature as a white man from the plantocracy who elected Western civilization as his home.[7] This ambivalent relationship is reenacted in Chamoiseau's character, an African and now Caribbean man, who inhabits the name of the slave trader captain, which fell upon him via the shoulder harness engraved with the ship captain's name, left with him on the island. May we then read the stranded human as Patrick Chamoiseau and the ship's captain as Saint-John Perse?

The stage of "The Idiot," "of a Western dimension," reminds us of the hubris of the "white world," expressed by Aimé Césaire in his *Notebook of a Return to the Native Land:* "Listen to the white world . . . its stiff joints crack under the hard stars / hear its blue steel rigidity pierce the mystic flesh."[8] Like in Césaire's "white world," Western conquest, for Chamoiseau, is undeniably connected to the rape of the land's "flesh." In Chamoiseau's *Crusoe,* the rape of the flesh, the rape of the island, gain an Anthropocenic dimension. As historians of science, Christophe Bonneuil and Jean-Baptiste Fressoz encapsulate it: "The

Anthropocene is the sign of our power, but also of our impotence."[9] In his colonizing madness, Sapiens is an idiot.

The Little Person: Small Is Big

Twenty-years after being cast off on the island, Crusoe's obsessive need to exploit and conquer dwindles. His disenchantment makes him relinquish Western hubris and even his humanity. The billy goat he encounters holds, in Crusoe's eyes, more humanity than himself: "*this old goat had looked much more human than I did . . .*" (56). Crusoe realizes the smallness of his being among the overwhelming strength of his surroundings: "thus the idiot I had become after all these years may have transformed into . . . a small person" (107). The humility expressed in the phrase "petite personne" also signals a return to a stage of childhood wonder. "Petite personne" can be read as a linguistic calque of the Creole expression *ti moun,* which simply means "a child," who is in the world to marvel and to learn from the "adult" or *gwan moun* who is the *entour:* "while rediscovering the island, the impression that grew in my mind was one of 'fierce thickness,' a primordial state of which I perceived only a tiny bit, that cared little about my fortifications . . . the island existed here as it always had—huge, endless—and I thought I had domesticated it; I felt infinitesimal in front of such profusion" (61). Not only large in scale, animals and trees gain personhood and the power of speech: "the trees suddenly seemed alive; they connected in secret unions that I sometimes walked along in silence, I lowered my head so as not to disturb" (64). Crusoe's letting go of his superiority, paired with the trees gaining agency, reminds us of Chamoiseau's fellow Martinican Suzanne Césaire, who developed the theory of the Martinican person as "homme-plante" (human-plant) in her 1942 essay "Malaise d'une civilisation," originally published in the journal *Tropiques:*

> What is the Martinican?
> —A plant-human
> Like a plant, he abandons himself to the rhythm of universal life. There is not the slightest effort to dominate nature. Mediocre

farmer. Perhaps. I am not saying he makes the plant grow: I am saying that he grows, he lives in a plant-like manner . . . he lets himself be carried along by life, docile, light, un-insistent, non-rebellious—in a friendly way, lovingly.[10]

In his stage of "petite personne," Chamoiseau's Crusoe embraces this surrendering and amorous relation to the animate and inanimate beings that surround him. In a Deleuze and Guattarian mode of becoming animal, the man lets go of his human shell to be one among many. This is particularly striking in the marvelous event of countless turtles coming ashore to breed:[11] "then, I slipped down into, like the birds and crabs, the entanglement of shells . . ." (79). It is paradoxically his acceptance of smallness, and relinquishing of a fixed ontology in embracing becoming, that gives the man access to an immense, larger-than-human, time. Chamoiseau's elder Suzanne Césaire calls this mode of being an "abandon au rythme de la vie universelle," a letting go that we witness in the island human becoming turtle: "I understood that the turtles and I did not live in the same time; their lives here resulted from an endless slowness, of an eternal loop impossible to comprehend and that could have swallowed me whole had I wanted to grasp any meaning or some sort of outcome from it . . ." (80). Toward the end of the "The Small Person," the intriguing word "présences" repeats like a multiplying echo. This word becomes the site, or more exactly, the sites, of a multiple agency, which Crusoe had failed to find in another singular human being: "I found myself facing another self: the whole, entire island; I now perceived it like a multitude that touched me . . . presences! . . ." (105). We can recognize, in this episode, a manifestation of Glissant's Relation, a nonhierarchical, open, rhizomatic, "boundless," "never-ending" way of being-in-the-world.[12] For Chamoiseau. "each blade of grass, each ancestral tree or lack thereof . . . constituted a hosanna of enduring correlations" (106). Chamoiseau's relation is radically ecological. It embraces an *oikos,* a house that is not the imposition of a human structure on the landscape but the relinquishing of solid human walls in order to embrace the multiple, complex, and ever-changing shell combinations of sea turtles and other animated beings.

The Artist: Humanity Relinquished

If the epoch of "The Idiot" was teleological, if that of "The Small Person" was relational, the time of "The Artist" moves from cataclysmic to sacred. An earthquake and a rogue wave turn the landscape upside down, and silence the "presences" that had become the stranded man's companions. The fragile harmony between all the components of the *entour* is turned into shards: "I saw the scurrying swarms of ants, among countless creatures that were seemingly made of humus and small anxieties" (127). After an initial state of panic, the human regains an equilibrium that allows him to reach a new ecological state, finding a home with multiple others in a constantly evolving system, as if the recognition of his utter vulnerability was precisely that which allowed him to take part in a Césairian model of "human-plant" and a Glissantian relational state: "I felt the frenzy of the trade winds, birds, bees, and rodents . . . anything motionless must certainly have been plants, but the most rooted plants also engage in incessant movement" (141). With his embrace of animal and plant rhythms, the human experiences "a freedom with no compromise that . . . gave me limitless access to myself and my surroundings; *a coming into relation*" (145). Chamoiseau qualifies this ecological relational attitude as "high consciousness."[13] Once more, and paradoxically, smallness as humility (as in humble, humus, closeness to the land), is what brings the human to its highest sphere.

The titular footprint, which had been, up to then, a constant warrant of the man's humanity, reverts back to an unmarked, primordial state: "the clay was now bluish . . . and spotted with black stuff similar to potter's clay . . . it could have very well been inhuman" (131). All Robinsonades, Chamoiseau reminds us in "The Footprint Workshop," represent a process of humanization and individuation: "The 'Crusoe adventure' is an archetype of individuation; this is why the story continues to fascinate us, it is ever inexhaustible" (159). Paradoxically, in Chamoiseau's footprint, individuation and humanization are reached only as the human individual relinquishes its solid walls. Becoming less human is also becoming more human, in a relational, ecological, aesthetic, and sacred embrace of the world.

On his last day on the island, which is also the last page of the narrative, the no-longer-stranded human becomes a high priest devoted to the *entour,* cultivating himself and the island with an aesthetic touch: "I peacefully continued my ceremony of the winds . . . I made sure to don a few nice necklaces, very fine animal pelts, to braid the hair that to fell to my shoulders and perfume it with cinnamon" (150). This veneration of the winds associated with a respectful production of beauty through adornments and perfumes appears as the antithesis of the teleological drive of possessing the land of "The Idiot" phase.[14] Such an offering of beauty and veneration to the *entour* is markedly performed in Chamoiseau's own *Crusoe's Footprint,* whose meticulous, careful, dense, opaque, exacting, and ultimately exquisite language is put to the service of making us aware of our reckless ecological footprint.

Captain's Log: The Final Word?

In the final and longest extract from the "Captain's Log," we learn that the very captain who had abandoned the human is eager to return to observe, with a perverse scientific mind, the living laboratory he had fathered on the island: "Returning was an adventure that I enjoyed leading. I had in this way sowed many islands with chickens, pigs, and at times even rats inadvertently . . . It allowed us to lightly sow these deserted lands with meat" (151). This individual drive to alter the world for selfish pleasure can also be read as a miniature of the beginning of the human-triggered Anthropocene, which, according to some recent theories, coincides with the conquest and colonization of the so-called New World.[15]

The slow ecological time the human had felt with the *entour* in his decades-long sojourn precipitates into a brutal and murderous time in the few hours that follow his "retrieval." The readers learn that the stranded human had been African, more specifically a Dogon from the Saharan region of West Africa. This, we learn only through the captain's "white gaze," to use a

Fanonian expression, without which the man is simply human: "His head was covered in long braids like a pharaoh. . . . He was dressed in animal pelts . . . in the tradition of his people and land. . . . He talked . . . in spirals, as one could hear in the traditional rhetoric of griots in villages of Negritia. . . . There was no longer any trace of that young Dogon sailor, educated from the Quran and Egyptian texts. . . . his name was Ogomtemmêli, son of a line of great knowledgeable hunters . . ." (153).

Captain Crusoe's account reveals his sensitivity to the language, poetry, and culture of his captive. It is surprising to hear that a ship captain has an understanding of the oral spirals of the griots. In this ethnographic portrait from the captain's log, we can discern the voice of Chamoiseau, who portrays the man in all his cultural, aesthetic, religious, historical, and philosophical depth. The name Ogomtemmêli inscribes the human into a historical moment. Ogotemmêli was a sage, scholar, and erudite Dogon who helped the French ethnographer Marcel Griaule understand the cosmogony and human systems of the Dogon world.[16] Ogotemmêli contributed to the improvement and expanse of European ethnography on Africans. The dignified humanity contained in the name offers a sharp contrast with the treatment of Ogomtemmêli by the captain and his men. To suppress Ogomtemmêli's revolutionary will to liberate the enslaved Africans in the hold, the captain "had him chained with our [human] merchandise . . . stocked in the hold" (154) and then abandoned on the island. Upon his return on the ship, Ogomtemmêli experiences his individual and collective trauma all over again and demands for "the hold to be opened" in a wish "to free the captives and bring them with him to the island" (156). His insurrection and cry for freedom are met with a cowardly murder: "alas we were forced to shoot him from afar. I was very sad because of this misfortune" (156). The passive and fatalistic turns of the sentences ("alas we were forced," "misfortune") are typical of the disengagement of their responsibility in the crime of slavery by white men. The affect of the captain ("I was very sad") is what has been explained in contemporary theories of white "sadness" in the face of our own crimes.[17] The captain's cowardice is even stronger in light of the partnership, friendship, even brotherhood that the two had developed: "The young sailor, educated from the Quran and Egyptian texts and skilled at almost everything" was the captain's teacher as well: "I had taught him everything I knew, and he had passed on just as much to me" (153). Ogomtemmêli had educated Captain Crusoe in a way similar to how Ogotemmêli had taught Marcel Griaule.

Another doubling constant in the text is the Crusoe-Ogomtemmêli pair echoing the one formed by Saint-John Perse and Chamoiseau. "It's sad," we could paraphrase Chamoiseau, "Saint-John Perse was a planter and a proponent of the West." Indeed, Saint-John Perse is at once a creator of beauty, a Caribbean model for Chamoiseau, and a champion of the West and its ideals. This ambivalent relationship between the Martinican writer of African origin and the Guadeloupean poet born of a lineage of white plantocracy is made even more tortuous when, in a final reversal of fortune, the ship's captain finds himself stranded on a deserted island, sole survivor of a shipwreck: "I did not know that I would now have to undergo what my unfortunate victim had just experienced before me, as if by prophecy, using my name" (157). In this illustration of teleology gone awry, the conqueror, in his search for expanse and progress encounters inconceivable time: "Now . . . lost on a similar island, these first words that I am writing in my poor logbook are for him, to ask for forgiveness, but also to position my survival in line with his strange experience" (157). It is dizzying to imagine the temporal structure of *Crusoe's Footprint:* the entrenching narrative (Crusoe) now becomes entrenched in the captain's journal; time is turned on its head when the past precedes the present (Defoe's narrative begins at the end of Chamoiseau's chronologically ulterior narrative). Like the *entour,* time is a conundrum that humans cannot seize. Chamoiseau himself gets sucked into his own text when he ends it with the inscription "Favorite, March 2008–July 2010" (158), as if he, himself, was keeping a journal, an account of time. This marking of date and place is reminiscent of the entries in the "Captain's Log" such as "July 22—In the year of our Lord 1659—These journeys to the New World" (7). The man on the island of Martinique, la

Favorite being Chamoiseau's street address in the town of La-
mentin, is at once part of the maddening lineage of writers of
Robinsonades, and outside of them. As a Martinican ecological
writer, Chamoiseau's stance is quite the opposite of "inseminating the island." Instead, the island pollinates him as he becomes
one germinating particle among so many others.

The end of *Crusoe's Footprint* puzzles. Judging by the murder of Ogomtemmêli, the zero-footprint human, we could in-
fer that the Anthropocene will go on after the murder of the
sustainable human. An alternative ending is also possible. The
captain, upon examination of the island, observes: "The island
seemed intact, neither fields, nor pipes nor mills. . . . I did not
find any trace whatsoever of human life that would have subsisted here over all these years. It was only an island of forgotten times and fixed eternities. As for the footprint, we could not
find it anywhere" (157). Since the readers do not know whether
Ogomtemmêli erased all signs of his presence or if the island
itself wiped them away, Chamoiseau leaves us with a mixed
ending. Should we be celebrating Ogomtemmêli's zero footprint
achievement or lamenting the planet's success in erasing us humans (as a consequence of our own Anthropocenic acts)? It
is not surprising that Chamoiseau leaves us with an unsolved
enigma, perhaps implying that the future is not fatalistic but
is in our hands. This last message is crucial in this moment of
our history when our brutal treatment of the planet for our
own progress threatens to end our species, and so many others,
by making it uninhabitable. "The health of humankind is the
reflection of the health of the planet" (147) proclaims a sibylic
voice in "The Artist" section. Planet Earth will go on without
us and our footprint, should the Crusoes of the world win over
the Ogomtemmêlis.

Notes

1. On Chamoiseau's ecological thinking and practice, see Hannes
de Vriese, who reflects on ecopoetics and natural disasters ("Écritures
antillaises entre géopoétique et écopoétique: Sur la nature des
cataclysmes chez Patrick Chamoiseau et Daniel Maximin," *Revue*

critique de fixxion française contemporaine 11 [2015]: 16–27); Renée Gosson, who examines intersections between the loss of Creole culture and ecological devastation in Martinique ("For What the Land Tells: An Ecocritical Approach to Patrick Chamoiseau's 'Chronicle of the Seven Sorrows,'" *Callaloo* 26, no. 1 [2003]: 219–34); and Richard Watts, who reveals "the conjuncture of two approaches—ecocritical and postcolonial" in Chamoiseau's works ("Poisoned Animal, Polluted Form: Chamoiseau's Birds at the Limits of Allegory," *Pacific Coast Philology* 46, no. 2 [2011]: 177–93, on 177).

2. Michel Tournier, *Vendredi, ou les limbes du Pacifique* (Paris: Gallimard, 1967). On Chamoiseau's *Crusoe's Footprint* in relation to his predecessors (Daniel Defoe, Saint-John Perse, Michel Tournier, and J. M. Coeetze), see Isabelle Constant's *Le Robinson antillais: De Daniel Defoe à Patrick Chamoiseau* (Paris: L'Harmattan, 2015), esp. 129–39.

3. Malcom Ferdinand reveals the imbrication between the violence of slavery and that of the Anthropocene in his interdisciplinary and erudite *Une écologie décoloniale:* "The European colonization of the Americas is only another name for the infliction, in such a singular, violent, and destructive way, of inhabiting the earth" (Paris: Seuil, 2019), 67.

4. See Glissant's *Philosophie de la Relation* (Paris: Gallimard, 2009) and Carrie Noland's "Édouard Glissant: A Poetics of the Entour," in *Poetry After Cultural Studies,* ed. Heidi R. Bean and Mike Chasar (Iowa City: University of Iowa Press, 2011), 143–72.

5. Chamoiseau offers a theoretical reflection on the enmeshment of Western supremacy over fellow humans with the depletion of world resources in his *Frères migrants* (Paris: Seuil, 2017). The epoch he calls "le règne de Sapiens, dévastateur majeur" (85–96, 87) is antithetical to Glissant's movement and principle of Relation. An "Ecoystème relationnel," an aesthetic and ethical stance, would nullify the discarding and downright killing of migrants who lose their life at sea. "Les migrances" would become "une des forces de la Relation" (96).

6. Paul Valéry, "The Crisis of the Mind" (1919), in *Paul Valéry: An Anthology,* ed. James R. Lawler (London: Routledge, 1977) 94–107, on 94.

7. See Valérie Loichot, "Saint-John Perse's Imagined Shelter: 'J'habiterai mon nom,'" in *Discursive Geographies*, ed. Jeanne Garane (Amsterdam: Rodopi, 2005), 91–102.

8. Aimé Césaire, *Notebook of a Return to the Native Land*, trans. Clayton Eshleman and Annette Smith (Middletown, Conn.: Wesleyan University Press, 2001).

9. Christophe Bonneuil and Jean-Baptiste Fressoz, *The Shock of the Anthropocene: The Earth, History, and Us* (London: Verso, 2016).

10. Suzanne Césaire, *The Great Camouflage*, trans. Keith L. Walker (Middletown, Conn.: Wesleyan University Press, 2012).

11. Gilles Deleuze and Félix Guattari, "Becoming Animal," in *The Animals Reader: The Essential Classical and Contemporary Writings*, ed. Linda Kalof and Amy Fitzgerald (Oxford: Berg, 2007), 37–50.

12. Édouard Glissant, *Poetics of Relation*, trans. Betsy Wing (Ann Arbor: University of Michigan Press, 2000).

13. "Ecological consciousness is part of what could be called high consciousness" (Chamoiseau in "L'écriture de la nature ou le texte vivant: Hannes De Vriese s'entretient avec Patrick Chamoiseau," *Revue critique de fixxion française contemporaine* 11 [2015]: 128–32, on 128).

14. On beauty at the service of the environment in Chamoiseau, see Louise Hardwick, "Autour du rocher du diamant: Chamoiseau et la démarche écocritique," in *Patrick Chamoiseau et la mer des récits*, ed. Pierre Soubias et al. (Bordeaux: Presses universitaires de Bordeaux, 2017),189–204, on 203. Chamoiseau himself connects his aesthetic practice to an ethical, and we might add political, commitment: "My books are founded on an aesthetics, a poetics, but also an ethics" ("De Vriese s'entretient," 128).

15. The British geographers Simon Lewis and Mark Maslin have singled out the European conquest of the Americas as the beginning of the Anthropocene ("Defining the Anthropocene," *Nature*, 12 March 2015, 171–80). On the effect of the mixing "old" and "new" worlds species as an Anthropocenic force (cf. Chamoiseau's captain "inseminating" the islands), see Bonneuil and Fressoz: "The unification of the flora and fauna of the Old and New Worlds caused an upheaval in the agricultural, botanical and zoological map of the globe, newly mingling in a biological globalization forms of life

separated 200 million years earlier with the break-up of Pangaea and the opening of the Atlantic Ocean" (*Shock of the Anthropocene*, 25).

16. See Marcel Griaule, *A Conversation with Ogotemmêli* (London: Oxford University Press, 1965; originally published in 1948 as *Dieu d'eau*).

17. See, for instance, Robin DiAngelo's *White Fragility: Why It's So Hard for White People to Talk about Racism* (Boston: Beacon Press, 2018).

TRANSLATORS' NOTE

It is in an ethereal haze that Chamoiseau's *L'empreinte à Crusoé* opens, inviting the reader to embark upon a saga across the sea, over land, and through time. One enters into a space defined by none of those aforementioned boundaries—disoriented and squinting, blinking both to adjust to the bright light and to regain consciousness. The sweeping usage of pluperfect in the narration propels us further back into the story, blurring yesterday and years ago, past centuries and . . . present. This retelling, or rather, alternative narrative, of the classic tale encapsulates what myriad slaves underwent as they struggled to make sense of their own present. Wrested from their homelands and forced into shackles aboard ships, surviving the Middle Passage only to be cast into servitude in faraway lands among strangers, their histories, cultures, and languages lost, with little to cling to, succumbing to erasure or to being documented and retold through the eyes and ears of those in power. In such a mystified state, these souls adrift grappled to comprehend their reality as well as their own identity.

Chamoiseau's Crusoe discovers the island abandoned, which implicitly forces the reader to consider what befell the indigenous populations of the Caribbean. He has no choice but to recreate an identity for himself as many did before him, using the few resources he can recover from the shipwreck. Part of this selfhood is reflected in Chamoiseau's unorthodox writing style. Semicolons punctuate his sentences, which are strung together with commas and dashes. For Chamoiseau, the semicolon represents "the idea of stream of consciousness" (*Empreinte*, 161). This narrative technique allows the reader to access Crusoe's thoughts as they unfold in his mind, namely, the rhythm, the breaks, the repetitions, and the silences. As for following the rules of capitalization? Perhaps if the narrator had learned or deemed it a proper noun—perhaps not. One must bear in mind that the reader is not the final arbiter. We will mention, however, that the singular, first-person pronoun *je* is not capitalized in French, nor is *dieu*, "God." Ultimately, we decided to follow standard English practice. In stark contrast to Crusoe's language is that of the captain. He affixes dates to his log entries and adheres to the erudite conventions of spelling and punctuation. He details purposeful maneuvers and is fully aware of his command. The captain's tone is calm, collected, and in control, whereas Crusoe, while offering vivid descriptions, seems to feel his way about the world in a state of confusion and uncertainty with intermittent occasions of lucidity. Crusoe invents words that he cannot remember or lacks the vocabulary for as well (e.g., hopefoolness, toadpole, dwarfback, wreckeyage). This brings us to the Word, which holds far more significance than what its mere four letters might allude to.

Crusoe vacillates between being plagued by his absence of origin and being liberated by it. He goes on to evoke a new identity and is reborn by way of *le verbe*, or "the word." He remarks, *au départ de toutes les origines est le verbe*, "at the beginning of all origins is the word" (*Empreinte*, 38; 20). We distinguish "word," the combinations of letters that form meaningful units, from "Word." The latter refers to the form of human expression extending beyond comprehension and is meant to bespeak one's own agency. Expression therefore, can be scribed in ink, in dirt, or in the passing breeze . . . That others understand anyone's personal expression is not a requirement, nor is it always appropriate; the language and symbols that constitute human expression echo the governing principles that one harbors deep within. Amid peoples and cultures, the Word manifests itself in ritual and customs, venerated and handed down from generation to generation. Thus the Word carries a heavy load; laden in the Word is that history, culture, and language.

The beauty of Chamoiseau's Word lies in its exactness as well as its imprecision. The term *savane* (Creole: *savann*), for example, is preferred to the continental French *pré* for "field" or "meadow" in the French Caribbean. This one word conjures images of the African savanna ecosystem for English and French speakers alike; yet in French, the word choice immediately situates us in the West Indies. In contemporary terms, *savane* refers to a town's central square or a public park such as La place de la Savane in Fort-de-France, Martinique. Since no comparable word in English geolocates quite as *savane* does, we may have suffered a loss in translation but made a gain in universality. Other lexical clues can be found in the fauna and flora that Crusoe encounters. English nomenclature periodically restricts us to less colorful terminology or may afford us a faithful parallel: *oiseaux-mouches* to "hummingbirds," *poisson-boa* to "scaly dragonfish." Modern proofreaders paint red lines below "seagrapes," suggesting that we use two words; *bois d'Inde*, native to the West Indies, emerges as the "bay rum tree." Set against "kapok tree," *fromager* can commonly refer to a variety of trees and evokes imagery of tall roots and ropelike vines. Anchored in the Latin of scientific names complemented by the advent of image searches, these references invite us on a journey of the senses, dangling a line into the Crusoe's world from our own.

The verb *saisir* means "grasp" or "take hold of." Ironically, this verb and its noun form, *saisie,* proved to be a slippery signature phrase in the text. This word alone entails quite the nuanced concept, which led to much deliberation and finally a consultation with Chamoiseau himself. He draws a distinction from Stevenson's "tale" and Faulkner's "narrative," which allows us to perceive the unknown from reality, capturing existential moments in various states of existence. With a precise match for "grasp" in English, we chose to lean into the concept of perception; a mental snapshot or glimpse into one's psyche. Furthermore, these circumstances emphasize the processing that occurs between states of consciousness. We liken it to our own process of discovering the intricate nature of this word, for instance, forcing us to think twice about whether we are grasping physically or figuratively.

The originality of Chamoiseau's text emanates from his narrative structure: it is a prelude to Daniel Defoe's Robinson Crusoe, ending where Defoe's novel begins. This reverse chronology has a dual effect. First, it points out power relations in the yield of narratives about colonialism's past. Chamoiseau challenges his readers to ponder: whose story should be told first? In the act of recounting the slave trade, Chamoiseau elevates the perspective of enslaved Africans above the account of the slave trader or the colonizer. This deliberate authorial decision calls into question the primacy of European production of historical narratives. Second, it casts doubt upon the legitimacy of Defoe's novel as the origin of the Crusoe myth. Despite being written three centuries later, Chamoiseau's Robinson Crusoe appears before Defoe's, as if the origin "is ahead of us" (*Empreinte*, 164). Drawing on the philosophers Heidegger and Edgar Morin, Chamoiseau calls for the necessity to imagine new beginnings rather than follow the same literary paths and traditions. The origin is thereby an act of creation.

Another compelling stylistic addition to the text is "The Footprint Workshop," which is a twenty-page section added after the conclusion of the text. This collection of lines and notes offers invaluable insight into the author's construction of the novel. Chamoiseau notably reveals his fascination for Daniel Defoe and Michel Tournier, as well as crediting Pascal, Saint-John Perse, Derek Walcott, Édouard Glissant, and Morin as influences on the realization of *L'empreinte à Crusoé*, yet also leaves us to wonder about the masculinity of the Crusoe world. The discourse feels almost intimate and reads as if jotted on the first available piece of paper in pencil—perhaps because they read like internal monologue. Chamoiseau writes, "The most beautiful impulse comes from impossibility. We should spend time with this beauty—or rather let it surprise us" (171). As succinct as this phrasing may be, we took the time to process and convey the essence of his words. This section welcomes us to spend time in Chamoiseau's *Sentimenthèque*, or "Feelibrary," a guiding light from Crusoe's island to our world and back.

We conclude with a passage from Chamoiseau's "Workshop" in acknowledgment that this particular translation reflects our interpretation and perceptions. While no translation is perfect, language, like music, is universal. After careful consideration, we made language choices in accordance with Chamoiseau's original score; at times in unison, at times in harmony, but never in dissonance. Chamoiseau says, "There are always way too many words. One must spend hours and days reading and re-reading to find the word in excess. Each word cut deserves a trophy; sometimes, the sentence becomes too dry and they come back in force and are happy to do so . . . Musicality has the final say" (166).

Jeffrey Landon Allen and Charly Verstraet
Washington, DC, and Birmingham, Alabama

TRANSLATOR'S ACKNOWLEDGMENTS

While the myth of Robinson Crusoe revolves around a one-person narrative, this book would never have come to be without a kind, resourceful, and thoughtful community. This translation was undertaken in the midst of an unpredictable pandemic that upended our world. As COVID-19 forced us into isolation, the story of Crusoe alone on his own island felt even more compelling and relevant to our contemporary challenges. Despite solitary isolation, this translation thrived on solidarity. This translation has crossed the desks of many people in many places, and we will remain indebted to those whose contributions are incalculable in value.

This network of scholars, colleagues, and friends read excerpts, provided suggestions, and initiated conversations that fueled the inspiration behind this translation. First and foremost, we would like to thank John Maddox and Maria Antonia Anderson de la Torre, colleagues at the University of Alabama at Birmingham, for their invaluable feedback on the original project of this book translation. Carrie Noland, Nathan Dize, and Michael Garval graciously agreed to review excerpts and propose critical and transformative comments that shaped the final version of this translation. Charly's colleagues at the University of Alabama at Birmingham created the ideal environment for this book and have offered constant encouragement and fruitful discussions. They include Julián Arribas, Margaret Bond, Catherine Daniélou, Roberto Mayoral Hernández, John K. Moore Jr., Carolina Rodríguez Tsouroukdissian, and Lourdes Sánches-López. Thank you to cherished friends who have morally supported this endeavor and enriched conversations about Caribbean writers and translators: Franck

Andrianarivo Rakotobe, Jennifer Boum Make, Corine Labridy, Erika Serrato, Jocelyn Sutton Franklin, and Lucy Swanson.

We are grateful to have had the enthusiastic support of the University of Virginia Press. From the outset of this adventure, Eric Brandt has been eager to advance this project and has truly exceeded our expectations. Renée Larrier and Mildred Mortimer, editors of the CARAF series, have been earnest and encouraging throughout. Ruth Melville, whose sharp eye thoroughly examined the translation, was essential in improving the rhythm and narrative. Thank you to our managing editor, Ellen Satrom, who oversaw the project through to publication. In addition, we were fortunate to have two outstanding readers who provided extremely helpful comments at every stage of the peer-review process and assisted with translation strategies and decisions. Thank you to Patrick Chamoiseau for his passionate assistance and vigorous guidance, which enlightened us on the wealth and abundance of his writing. Thank you to Valérie Loichot, who eagerly accepted our invitation to write an eloquent and insightful afterword.

Furthermore, Charly would like to conclude his acknowledgments with his translation partner and his family. To Jeff, whose bright and lively spirit lifts mountains, you were the perfect companion on this long and winding road. To my parents, Laurent and Christine Verstraet, whose affection and encouragement can be felt from an ocean away. To my brothers and sisters: Shane, Laëtitia, Laurie, Johnny, and Maxime, who showed me the love and support of a large family throughout the translation. To my children: my son Léo, who, despite his young age, has become the family's official interpreter; my daughter Aléna, whose contagious smile shines while reading books on our little island; and to my son Luka, who rocked in my arms as I continually searched for the perfect words. Finally, thank you to my wife, Paula Verstraet, who dove into my fascination with Patrick Chamoiseau and his Robinson Crusoe, and who has been present at every stage of this book. She makes everyday life a beautiful journey.

Finally, Jeff wishes to express his appreciation to those near and dear to him. To his family, biological and chosen, without whose moral support and encouragement many accomplishments may not have been possible: Your words, your affection, your sustenance, and your patience contributed significantly to the progression of this work. To Sylvia and Carroll, who have tirelessly supported pursuits from adolescence into adulthood does Jeff extend his heartfelt gratitude. To Jonathan and Joshua, whose technological acumen throughout their formative years fostered international connections that developed into meaningful, lifelong relationships. To Aakib, whose art for painting words helped color the lines of this text, and for the consequential display of patience and support that served as an anchor. To Charly, who maintained the wind in the sails and kept course, any crewmate would be honored to have you as captain. To the countless others who constitute the priceless, vast network of support, may your names transcend these words of acknowledgment.

BIBLIOGRAPHY

Barnabé, Jean, Patrick Chamoiseau, and Raphaël Confiant. *Éloge de la créolité*. Paris: Gallimard, 1989.

———. *Éloge de la créolité / In Praise of Creoleness*. Translated by M. B. Taleb-Khyar. Paris: Gallimard, 1993. (First published in *Callaloo* 13, no. 4 [Fall 1990] : 886–909.)

Chamoiseau, Patrick. *À bout d'enfance*. Paris: Gallimard, 2006.

———. *Au temps de l'antan: Contes du pays Martinique*. Paris: Hatier, 1988.

———. *Biblique des derniers gestes*. Paris: Gallimard, 2002.

———. *Césaire, Perse, Glissant, les liaisons magnétiques*. Paris: Philippe Rey, 2013.

———. *Childhood*. Translated by Carol Volk. Lincoln: University of Nebraska Press, 1999. Originally published as *Antan d'enfance* (Paris: Hatier, 1990; Gallimard, 1993).

———. *Chronicle of the Seven Sorrows*. Translated by Linda Coverdale. Lincoln: University of Nebraska Press, 1999. Originally published as *Chronique des sept misères* (Paris: Gallimard, 1986).

———. *Le commandeur d'une pluie*. Paris: Gallimard, 2002.

———. *Contes des sages créoles*. Paris: Seuil, 2018.

———. *Le conteur, la nuit et le panier*. Paris: Seuil, 2021.

———. *Creole Folktales*. Translated by Linda Coverdale. New York: New Press, 1994.

———. *Un dimanche au cachot*. Paris: Gallimard, 2007.

———. *Écrire en pays dominé*. Paris: Gallimard, 1997.

———. *Émerveilles*. Paris: Gallimard, 1998.

———. *L'empreinte à Crusoé*. Paris: Gallimard, 2012.

———. *French Guiana: Memory-Traces of the Penal Colony*. Translated by Matt Reeck. Middletown, Conn.: Wesleyan University Press, 2020. Originally published as *Guyane: Traces-mémoires du bagne* (Paris: Caisse nationale des monuments historiques et des sites, 1994).

———. *From the Plantation to the City*. Translated by Jeffrey Landon Allen and Charly Verstraet. In *Black Shack Alley*, edited by Joseph Zobel. New York: Penguin Random House, 2020.

———. *Hypérion victimaire, Martiniquais épouvantable*. Paris: Éditions Labranche, 2013.

———. *Livret des villes du deuxième monde*. Paris: Patrimoine, 2002.

———. *Manman Dlo contre la fée Carabosse*. Paris: Éditions Caribéennes, 1982.

———. *La matière de l'absence*. Paris: Seuil, 2016.

———. *Migrant Brothers*. Translated by Matthew Amos and Fredrik Rönnbäck. New Haven, Conn.: Yale University Press, 2018. Originally published as *Frères migrants* (Paris: Seuil, 2017).

———. *Les neuf consciences du malfini*. Paris: Gallimard, 2009.

———. *Le papillon et la lumière*. Paris: Philippe Rey, 2011.

———. *School Days*. Translated by Linda Coverdale. Lincoln: University of Nebraska Press, 1997. Originally published as *Chemin d'école* (Paris: Gallimard, 1994).

———. *Seven Dreams of Elmira: A Tale of Martinique*. Translated by Mark Polizzotti. Cambridge, Mass.: Zoland Books, 1999. Originally published as *Elmire des sept bonheurs: Confidences d'un vieux travailleur de la distillerie Saint-Étienne* (Paris: Gallimard, 1998).

———. *Slave Old Man*. Translated by Linda Coverdale. New York: New Press, 2018. Originally published as *L'esclave vieil homme et le molosse* (Paris: Gallimard, 1997).

———. *Solibo Magnificent*. Translated by Rose-Myriam Réjouis and Val Vinokurov. New York: Pantheon, 1998. Originally published as *Solibo magnifique* (Paris: Gallimard, 1988).

———. *Texaco*. Translated by Rose-Myriam Réjouis and Val Vinokurov. New York: Pantheon, 1998. Originally published as *Texaco* (Paris: Gallimard, 1992).

———. *Veilles et merveilles créoles: Contes du pays Martinique*. Paris: Le Square, 2013.

Chamoiseau, Patrick, and Raphaël Confiant. *Lettres créoles. Tracées antillaises et continentales de la littérature: Haïti, Guadeloupe, Martinique, Guyane: 1635–1975*. Paris: Hatier, 1991.

Chamoiseau, Patrick, and Édouard Glissant. *L'intraitable beauté du monde: Adresse à Barack Obama*. Paris: Galaade, 2009.

Chamoiseau, Patrick, and Édouard Glissant. "When the Walls Fall: Is National Identity an Outlaw?" Translated by Jeffrey Landon Allen and Charly Verstraet. *Contemporary French and Francophone Studies*, 22, no. 2 (2018): 259–70. Originally published as *Quand les murs tombent: L'identité nationale hors-la-loi* (Paris: Galaade, 2007).

The Other Side of the Sea
Louis-Philippe Dalembert, translated by Robert H. McCormick Jr.

The Fury and Cries of Women
Angèle Rawiri, translated by Sara Hanaburgh

Far from My Father
Véronique Tadjo, translated by Amy Baram Reid

Climb to the Sky
Suzanne Dracius, translated by Jamie Davis

Land and Blood
Mouloud Feraoun, translated by Patricia Geesey

"At the Café" and "The Talisman"
Mohammed Dib, translated by C. Dickson

The Little Peul
Mariama Barry, translated by Carrol F. Coates

Aunt Résia and the Spirits and Other Stories
Yanick Lahens, translated by Betty Wilson

Above All, Don't Look Back
Maïssa Bey, translated by Senja L. Djelouah

*A Rain of Words: A Bilingual Anthology of Women's Poetry in
Francophone Africa*
Irène Assiba d'Almeida, editor, translated by Janis A. Mayes

The Abandoned Baobab: The Autobiography of a Senegalese Woman
Ken Bugul, translated by Marjolijn de Jager

Dog Days: An Animal Chronicle
Patrice Nganang, translated by Amy Baram Reid

The Land without Shadows
Abdourahman A. Waberi, translated by Jeanne Garane